Winter Sight

Book Two in the *Other Magic* Series

Nik DeKasha

ISBN 978-0-578-92395-6

Cover art by Raquel Sotomayor
Cover design by Mark Kregger

Printed in the United States of America

Titles in
the Other Magic series:

Winter Harvester
Winter Sight

*For my little birds, the four I cherish in this life
and the one I'll fly with in the next.*

One

Winnie pushed her choppy blond bangs off her forehead and reached up to knock on the door. Before she could, the bangs fell back into her eyes. Huffing, she pushed them up again. She raised her hand to knock once more, but paused, puffing up her cheeks and blowing out a whoosh of air before dropping her hand to her side. Her hair fell into her eyes again.

"Son of a—" she started, but her curse was cut short by the door suddenly flying open. Winnie took an unsteady step backward, her heel coming down on empty space. She pinwheeled her arms as she tipped backward off the top step. The man who had opened the door, a slight, dark-haired, olive-skinned stranger, leaped forward, his eyes opening in shock. He clutched her waving arms and yanked her forward, righting her footing on the concrete stoop.

"Are you okay?" he asked, concern creasing his forehead.

"Yeah, thanks," Winnie coughed out. She turned to look down the steep concrete steps behind her. "That would have hurt."

The man followed her gaze. "Yes, I can tell you from experience it does." Winnie looked at him curiously. "I learned the hard way last year. My first winter here."

Winnie snickered. "I guess I'm the second Winter here, then."

The man's eyebrows closed some of the distance to his hairline, and he pushed up his glasses with one finger. "I beg your pardon?"

"Never mind." Winnie felt her face flush with embarrassment. This wasn't how she'd planned for this meeting to take place. "Are you Nolan? Nolan Ramirez?"

"Ye-e-es," Nolan responded hesitantly, drawing out the word warily and tipping his head back a bit to peer down his nose at his mysterious visitor. He had to tip it pretty far back to achieve this since he was only a few inches taller than Winnie, who was diminutive herself.

Winnie thrust out her hand. "I'm Winnie Harvester. I'm friends with your sister, Nina."

Nolan took her hand out of habit and held it, but as he processed Winnie's greeting, a hard line formed between his dark eyes. Winnie loosened her grip to pull away, but Nolan tightened his hand on hers and leaned closer to her.

"You! You're the upstairs neighbor!" He wasn't yelling, exactly, but Winnie felt herself instinctively moving away from him.

"Well, yes...I...," she stammered, but he cut her off.

"Where is my sister? The last time I heard from her, she said she was going on a 'little trip' with her upstairs neighbor, and that was two and a half weeks ago!" Nolan dropped Winnie's hand to make air quotes around *little trip,* and Winnie used the opportunity to back away from him by stepping down a stair. "My sister never goes this long without contacting me," he went on. "So, where the hell is my sister?"

Winnie stood for a moment with her mouth working, thinking of the best way to respond to Nolan's perfectly reasonable questions. The problem wasn't that she didn't have answers for him; the problem was that the answers she had weren't believable. At least, they weren't going to sound believable to Nolan, who seemed to lack some of his sister's blithe open-mindedness.

"That's what I came here to talk to you about. It's kind of a long story. Can I come in? I promised Nina I'd answer all your questions before we, well, 'call' her." Winnie mimicked his use of air quotes around the word *call*.

"'Call' her?" More air quotes accompanied this, and Winnie hoped no one walking by on the street was watching the two of them stand in Nolan's doorway and waggle their fingers at each other. "What does that mean? Why can't I just call her the normal way? Where is she? Is she okay?" His voice rose again, and Winnie cursed herself for saying things all wrong. Nina had asked her to reassure Nolan, not to send him into a panic.

"Yes, she's fine. Better than fine, actually. She got a new job, and she's really enjoying it. The reason you haven't heard from her is…well…" Winnie faltered. The truthful explanation was that Nina was working in a place where time didn't operate quite the same way, so even though Nina had been gone only a few days on her end, Nolan's time had stretched much longer. But that probably wasn't the best way to start this explanation.

"She's in a place where there's no cell reception," she finished lamely.

Nolan stared at her.

"In another state," Winnie added. She left off *of existence* and wondered vaguely if that counted as dissembling. Nina wouldn't appreciate her lying to her brother.

Nolan looked at her skeptically, but finally he turned back to the door and pushed it open, stepping aside to invite her through.

Two

Winnie settled on the couch in Nolan's front room in front of a picture window that looked out on a tree-lined street flanked by brick townhomes largely identical to Nolan's. It was a quiet neighborhood, close enough to a main street to make city-living a walkable endeavor, but far enough from the buzzy activity of downtown to feel almost suburban.

After inviting her to sit, Nolan had disappeared into his kitchen to fetch them drinks, but Winnie noticed his head popping around the wall that separated the rooms every few seconds as if he was concerned she might suddenly decide not to explain anything and bolt out the front door. Or as if she might decide to slide some of his decorative, expensive-looking gewgaws—of which there were quite a few—into her purse. She gave him the benefit of the doubt and assumed it was the former.

She was smiling to herself, remembering a story Nina had told her when they'd first met about her knack for breaking breakable things and marveling at how different siblings could be when Nolan returned with two glasses of ice water and settled down across from her.

"What's funny?" he asked, and Winnie blushed.

"I was just thinking about Nina sitting here, surrounded by all these beautiful, fragile knickknacks," she told him honestly.

He looked around at the *objets d'art* littering the room's pristine surfaces and, to Winnie's surprise, chuckled. "Well, I normally don't leave her in this room unattended."

Winnie's smile turned to a frown while he was still looking around. Maybe he really had been keeping an eye on her for sticky fingers...

"So, where is she?" he asked her, getting back to business with lightning speed. Winnie bought herself a few more seconds by drinking deeply from the glass. With Verna's recent return, the intense, unseasonable heat had dissolved into a temperate spring, so she wasn't exactly parched from her trip across the city. But the various scenarios she'd imagined for this conversation had already fallen apart, and she was scrambling mentally for a new approach. What would Nina do if she were here?

Nolan cleared his throat, and Winnie met his irritated gaze over the top of her glass. She calmly set it on the coaster he'd set out for her and smoothed a nonexistent wrinkle from her skirt.

"Well, Nolan, I'm sure you have a lot of questions for me, and like I said, I promised Nina I'd answer them all."

"Yes, you've said that already. What I'm waiting for is an explanation of where my sister is and what you have to do with her ending up there."

"Me?"

"You. My sister told me she'd become friends with her upstairs neighbor and was helping her with some kind of search. Frankly, she was a bit cagey about the whole thing, and that's not like Nina."

"No, I agree."

"Then," he went on as if she hadn't spoken, "she told me she needed to accompany this neighbor on some kind of...I don't know, business trip. Something like that. And now it's been almost three weeks since I've heard from her, and here you show up on my front porch and tell me she's gone off to work in another state. Whatever's going on with my sister, Winnie, it sure seems to have started with you. So, I'd like to know what the hell is going on, and I'd like to know right now."

Winnie stared at Nolan with wide eyes; she wasn't afraid of him, but she hadn't prepared herself to be dressed down. The fact was she hadn't totally recovered from the events that had led to Nina taking on her new role, and she was feeling a bit raw. But when she considered Nolan's words logically, she had to admit that he was right: from his perspective, it all looked pretty dodgy, and she did owe him an explanation.

"Okay, fine," she said at last, collapsing back against the sofa. "The truth is your sister came along with me to find my sister, who had been kidnapped by this guy named Tod, who basically checks dead people in and out of the afterlife. But time there doesn't run at the same speed as it does here, in life, so we didn't think we were gone that long, which is why Nina didn't check in with you the last couple of weeks. Anyway, my sister ended up being fine—well, I don't know if *fine* is the right word: she's married to Tod now and having his baby, which didn't go over at all well with our parents, I can tell you. Honestly, I still don't know how I feel about the whole thing, but there's no going back now, so I suppose my feelings don't matter.

"Anyway, now my sister is back at her job here among the living—she makes the seasons turn from winter to spring—and Nina's keeping an eye on the afterlife as an interim coordinator so that Tod can live with her here and support her while she has their baby."

Nolan gaped at her when she'd stopped talking, and Winnie picked up her ice water and sipped it demurely.

"Seriously?" he asked.

"Yes. I mean it's been a little bit of a logistical nightmare, but she's got a kind of personal assistant helping her out while she learns the ropes. In fact, he—"

"Stay right there," Nolan interrupted her, rising. "I need to make a phone call."

"A phone call?" Winnie felt a frisson of unease as Nolan left the room. "Who are you calling?" she called after him.

"The police. I don't know what you've done with my sister, but if you can't be honest with me, I'm happy to let them deal with you."

Winnie was on her feet in an instant and racing to intercept Nolan. She caught up with him as he picked his cell up from the counter in the kitchen.

"Nolan, you can't!" she insisted, but when she looked into his face, she read...fear? Was that really fear in his expression? She shook herself.

It isn't fear of you, dummy. It's fear for his sister, she thought.

"I'm sure I sound like a lunatic." She chose to ignore his grunt of agreement. "Your sister accepted all this with total equanimity. I should have realized that not everyone would understand me the way she does."

Nolan was holding the phone and regarding Winnie warily, but she was relieved to see he hadn't dialed the police yet.

"Please hear me out, Nolan. I'm not crazy, and I'm not dangerous. More importantly, Nina is fine, and she's not in any trouble."

Nolan glanced at the phone, clearly weighing whether or not to make the call.

"You don't need to call the police!" Winnie all but yelled in Nolan's face, and he reared back, startled.

His face darkened, and he straightened. "If you're trying to prove you're not insane, you're doing a pretty bad job of it."

Winnie scrubbed her face with her hands and combed her hair out of her eyes with her fingernails.

"I know," she acknowledged. "I'm sorry. I've had a rough couple of weeks." She glanced around the small kitchen and, seeing a stool nearby, sat down heavily. "I promised Nina I'd come here and explain everything to you, and I'm messing it up." She smiled ruefully. "The irony is that if she were here, she'd know exactly what to say to you."

Winnie sat bolt upright, clapping a hand to her forehead. "Jeez. Why can't she?"

"Why can't she what?" Nolan asked, his eyes narrowing in suspicion.

"Why can't she explain everything?" Winnie hopped off the stool and reentered the kitchen. "Can you fill a shallow bowl with water?"

Nolan's eyes became, if possible, even more distrustful. "Why?" he asked.

Winnie grinned. "We're going to put in a very long-distance call to Nina."

Nolan was still grumbling under his breath when he sat down on the stool next to Winnie's at the high table, a pasta bowl filled to the halfway point with tap water between them.

"I can't believe I'm going along with this madness," he mumbled. "If you didn't seem exactly like the kind of person Nina would get herself wrapped up with, I'd have called the cops already." He scowled at Winnie. "Don't think I've ruled out the possibility, either."

Winnie flushed, but she repositioned the bowl between them without a word and took a few deep breaths.

"Ready?" she asked.

"Ready for what?" Nolan demanded impatiently. He might have Nina's dark eyes and tawny skin, but he definitely didn't have her devil-may-care approach to new experiences, Winnie thought ruefully.

"Just watch," she said. "Put your finger in the water." He muttered something that sounded a lot like *this is stupid*, but Winnie decided to channel Meri and pretend she hadn't heard.

She rested her hand beside the bowl opposite Nolan's and dipped one fingertip in the water. Then, she summoned her magic and whispered, "Show us Nina."

"What's that supposed…to…" Nolan trailed off as the water in the basin began to swirl. "How are you doing that?" he asked quietly.

"I'm not, really," Winnie answered. "I mean, I am in the sense that I'm using my power to make it happen, but I don't control how the process works. Actually, I didn't even know an anchor pool was a thing until a couple of days ago. The guy who uses these things, Tod, pretty much kept to himself until just recently, so I'm new to this, too."

Nolan smiled weakly, the way one might when meeting an ex's new partner in a very public place.

"Ah, I see."

Winnie was certain he didn't see at all, but it was only a few moments before the swirling water began to darken, and Nolan's attention was drawn back to the bowl. Winnie studied his face as he watched the swirling water: his nose was straight and narrow like Nina's, but his eyes were set wider apart. Behind his glasses, he had dark, thick lashes like Nina's too. His eyes were lighter than his sister's, hazel-brown, Winnie thought, instead of Nina's pure brown. Winnie resisted the urge to lean forward to look closely at the edges of his irises for fear her scrutiny might come across as further evidence of threatening instability.

Suddenly, Nolan snatched his hand away from the bowl, jumping off his stool so quickly that it fell backward and slammed onto the wood flooring with a crack like a gunshot.

"What the hell?" he cried, pointing at the bowl with his dripping finger.

Winnie looked down into the bowl and smiled. "Nina!" she exclaimed.

"Hi, Winnie!" Nina responded joyfully, her image rippling on the surface of the water. Winnie took her finger out of the water, and Nina's face flickered with the rings the disruption caused. "Did you find Nolan? Were you able to explain things?" she asked.

"I did one better, Nina." Winnie looked up at Nolan, who was still straddling the stool on the floor, watching Winnie with disbelief. "Come say hi, Nolan," she said, like a kindergarten teacher coaxing a bashful student to make a new friend.

"Nolan's there?" Nina squealed, and Winnie leaned closer to the bowl to whisper.

"I think he's freaking out a little. What should I say?"

"Tell him you know how hard this is to understand, but he should think about those bacteria that live underwater."

Winnie looked at her friend blankly, then chuckled. "Say that again, Nina? I thought you said something about bacteria."

Nina nodded vigorously. "I did. Just say it."

Winnie turned back to Nolan, who still stood frozen far from the bowl. "Nolan, Nina says she knows this is kind of nuts, but you should think about bacteria."

Nolan's brow creased in puzzlement, and Nina, listening to Winnie speak to her unseen brother, hissed,

"Not just bacteria, Winnie! The underwater bacteria he told me about."

"Oh! Sorry." Winnie grinned sheepishly. "She says think about the underwater bacteria you told her about."

"Bacteria?" Nolan repeated as if he'd never heard the word before.

Winnie turned back to Nina. "I don't think he knows what you mean," she reported.

"Okay, remind him that a few weeks ago, he sent me a text with a link to some article he found in a scientific journal about these bacteria…was it bacteria? Or maybe it was some kind of kelp?" Nina put her finger to her lips, screwing up her face thoughtfully.

Winnie sighed and looked up at Nolan. "Okay, look, if you want to talk to Nina, you're going to have to come over here and do it. This is like playing a game of telephone."

Nolan cleared his throat and bent to pick up the stool. He held it between himself and Winnie, and she had the ridiculous idea that he was going to clutch it by the seat and fend her off with it, like a lion-tamer in an old-timey cartoon.

Instead, he set it down at the bar and leaned hesitantly over the bowl. "Nina?"

"Hi, Nole!" Nina chirped happily. "Don't you remember that article you sent me?"

Winnie marveled at Nina's ability to treat any situation as if it were perfectly normal.

Unsurprisingly, Nolan didn't seem confused by *this* conversation.

"No, you'll have to refresh my memory. But before we discuss that, can you tell me why you're in a bowl of water and how I'm talking to you right now?"

"Yes," she responded. "I took a job as a transitions coordinator, but my office doesn't really get cell service. So now this is how you'll call me. And you do remember: it was about these bacteria that don't need to breathe."

Nolan closed his eyes and pinched the bridge of this nose. "They weren't bacteria; they were parasites. But actually, I need to go back for one second to the fact that you're in a bowl of water. Er...no, let's finish this out first: what does a deep-sea parasite have to do with your new job?" Nolan seemed a little afraid of the answer.

"Oh! Nothing. But when we talked about that article, you said that what made those little critters so amazing was that they shouldn't exist, and they made scientists rethink a lot of the ideas they were sure had to be absolute physical laws."

"Okay...?" Winnie thought she got the connection Nina was making but felt it would be churlish to jump in, like shouting out an answer in class when the other students were raising their hands.

"This is like that, Nolan. You thought you knew how the world worked, but Winnie is going to make you rethink all your ideas."

Nolan looked up at Winnie, who hadn't anticipated this turn in the conversation. He stared at her, and at a loss for what to say to make him feel better about having the metaphysical rug pulled out from under his feet, she raised one hand and chucked him on the arm.

"Heh…yeah," she said lamely, blushing under his stony stare. "Got any wine?"

It took most of the afternoon—and something a good deal stronger than wine for Nolan—for Winnie to tell the whole story, but by dinnertime, she felt she could at least leave safely without fear that he would call the police the moment the door closed behind her. Telling Nina about her true nature had been so easy that Winnie had been lulled into complacency; she hadn't anticipated how long it would take Nolan to understand and accept the things she told him. It didn't help that Nina had been available only for a few minutes before being called away by Abel, the soul-steward-turned-personal-assistant she'd mentioned to Nolan, leaving Winnie the responsibility of helping Nolan accept his sister's new reality all on her own.

As Winnie rode home in a cab that evening, she reflected the day. Nolan had seemed to go through the five stages of grief in just a few hours. He'd denied the possibility of what she was telling him, and then railed at her for dragging his sister into a perilous situation and leaving her to report to a dangerous kidnapper. He'd suggested alternatives for Nina staying in the afterlife, even after Winnie had assured him that Nina was perfectly happy with the work. At hearing this, he'd slumped unhappily in his chair, nursing his drink morosely and brooding. Finally, he'd sighed and risen, carrying his tumbler and her not-quite-empty wine glass to the kitchen. Winnie had taken that as the sign that it was time for her to leave.

Now, laying her head back against the headrest, she closed her eyes. The last few days since she, Tod, and Verna had returned from the Depths had been a whirlwind. She'd spent every waking minute refereeing the showdowns between Verna and Brooke, Pete and Tod, Brooke and Pete, Autumn and Verna, and seemingly every other combination of all parties involved. The one peaceful family member in all of this was Meri, whose indefatigable happiness—and recent addition of a new girlfriend—meant she welcomed Verna back with no questions asked and greeted Tod with open arms. As parents and husband and sisters fought and spit, Meri had settled back with her sketch pad and pencils, drawing a portrait of the newlyweds.

It wasn't until Verna had finally thrown up her hands in frustration and informed Tod they were leaving that Autumn had looked over Meri's shoulder and asked the question that had reignited the powder keg: "Meri, why does Vee look pregnant in this picture?"

Since then, to the best of Winnie's knowledge, Verna and Tod had been holed up at Verna's apartment, Brooke had refused to take calls or visitors, and Pete had been sleeping in one of his underground bunkers, a habit he employed from time to time when his excavations had him too far underground to make coming topside feasible or, as in this case, pleasant.

In short, the family was in chaos. And though it was Tod's—and Verna's, Winnie admitted, but mostly

Tod's—fault, Winnie couldn't help feeling some responsibility for introducing discord into their once-happy family. She sighed deeply.

As the cab neared home, though, she felt relief wash over her. It had been a long day to end a long week, but explaining everything to Nolan had been the last task she'd needed to cross off her to-do list. Now, it was done, and the wine she'd enjoyed all afternoon, combined with the prospect of a quiet evening at home, filled her with peaceful warmth. Tomorrow might bring a slew of new challenges, but for tonight, at least, her time would be entirely her own.

She got out at the curb when the cab pulled up at her building and climbed the stairs to her door. Once inside, she scanned Nina's door for packages or signs of trouble and, finding none, headed up the stairs to her apartment. Joyfully, she turned the key in the lock and stepped inside, sighing again at the thought of pouring one more glass of wine and tackling a book from her to-be-read stack.

"It sure feels good to be home," she said into the empty air, and then she nearly jumped out of her skin when the empty air talked back.

Three

"Must be nice," said a baritone voice from somewhere deeper in the apartment. Winnie stood inside the door, waiting for her heart to stop pounding out of control. She was startled, but she wasn't afraid. The voice was familiar.

"Tod, what are you doing in my apartment?" she demanded as she strode up the hallway toward the living room. When she entered, she found him sprawled on the couch, her remote lying on his chest and his thumbs working busily at a smartphone he held up over his face. Winnie waited for him to look up. He didn't.

"I see you've adapted to the technology of the living without a problem," she said wryly, heading to the kitchen to pour herself a glass of wine and a bowl of cereal.

From the other room, Tod only grunted.

Winnie sighed. "Seriously…why are you here?"

She heard the thump of the remote on her coffee table, and a moment later Tod was standing in the kitchen doorway.

"I needed to get away from Verna for a little while." He didn't look at her as he stood there, and she paused to study his face before pouring milk on her cereal.

When he finally made eye contact, his shoulders slumped and he groaned. "Fine. Verna told me to go find something to do for a few hours. She said she needed some breathing room."

Winnie began crunching, still watching Tod. When she swallowed, she said again, "Okay…but seriously, why are you *here*? It's a big city, Tod. Surely there are other places you could be besides my apartment?"

"Like where?" He seemed genuinely mystified.

"Umm...like a movie? A library? A bookstore? A park? Pretty much anywhere but my apartment? None of those places sound good to you?"

Tod squirmed. "I thought maybe you and I could..." He trailed off, and Winnie focused on taking several deep breaths. The Winnie of a year ago, who fretted over what people thought and how they might react, would have put a consoling arm around her brother-in-law and invited him to share his burden; the Winnie washing down shredded wheat with chardonnay, who had risked her personal wellbeing to travel to literal hell and back to rescue her sister, didn't feel quite so empathetic. That Winnie wanted a hot bath, a good book, and a total dearth of whiny, needy in-laws.

"Spit it out, Tod. I've had a long day."

Tod drew himself up, sensing Winnie's disinclination to sympathize. "I'm sorry if my marital discord is inconveniencing you, Winnie." Winnie didn't think he sounded very sorry. "I just thought you were the right person to ask for advice about Verna. It's not like I can go to anyone else in the family for help."

Winnie considered. Tod was right that no other Harvester was likely to offer tea and sympathy; there were a lot of hard feelings among all of them despite Verna's return. Did she owe it to Tod to support him now?

Hell no, a small but surprisingly ardent voice chirped inside her head. *Tell him you've met your dealing-with-other-people's-crises quota for the year.*

But there was Verna to consider. This wasn't just about Tod.

Winnie set her bowl down on the counter, her mind made up. "I'm happy to talk to you, Tod. I'm sure what you're going through right now is rough, and I've known Verna plenty long to know that she can be temperamental at the best of times. Who knows what she's like pregnant?"

Tod sighed with relief, a sedate smile turning up the corners of his mouth. "That's great, Winnie. I knew that if—"

"I'm not done," Winnie cut him off with a raised hand. "I'm happy to talk, but it's been a long few days, and I'm just beat. I don't have it in me to sort out anything with you tonight. More to the point, I didn't give you permission to come into my home when I wasn't here, and I don't like the position you've put me in."

Tod's eyes widened innocently. "I didn't mean anything by it, Winnie. Verna gave me the key. She said you wouldn't mind me coming in, that she does it all the time..."

"Well," Winnie answered, determined to stick to her guns, "it isn't up to Verna. This is *my* apartment, and I'm telling you that I don't want you coming in here without my knowledge."

She held out her hand. Tod stared at it blankly.

"Key?" Winnie prompted.

Tod jumped like he'd been poked and dug into his jeans pocket. He dropped the key into her upturned palm, his black eyes gazing at her balefully.

"Thank you," Winnie said. She tucked the key into the mail organizer on her counter to return to Verna later. *Along with a strong message about inviting people to treat her apartment like a flophouse,* the little voice in her head twittered again. This time she shushed it. She was enjoying her new, more assertive voice, but there was no call to get snippy.

"How about if we plan to meet for lunch tomorrow?" she suggested. "Tonight, I really need to relax and get a good night's sleep, but I don't have any lunch plans. Let's say noon?"

Tod assented, and she gave him the name and address of the café she and her sisters met at regularly. As she said it, she felt a little thrill at the thought that, for the first time in over a year, all four sisters would be reunited at this week's brunch.

Winnie walked Tod to her door and bade him goodnight. He looked at her mournfully, clearly hoping she'd relent and let him crash on her sofa, but Winnie refused to allow his puppy-dog gaze to change her mind. She had no idea where he'd sleep if Verna really had locked him out, and she had no intention of asking. When she'd closed the door behind him, she leaned against it.

"It sure feels good to be home," she said once again, holding her breath as the sound of her voice faded. This time, no one answered. She smiled and headed to the bathroom to run the bath.

Four

When Winnie awoke the next morning alone in her apartment, she cracked one eye in the direction of the warm glow from the drawn window shade and smiled. It was clearly mid-morning light, and she luxuriated in the knowledge that she didn't have to jump up and run off somewhere to save the day. Yes, her family was rife with discord, her first meeting with Nina's attractive brother had gone abominably, and she had a lunch date with the lord of the afterlife, but at least she'd gotten to sleep in. She punched her pillow to fluff it up, rolled over so that her back was to the window, and nestled back down into her cozy bedding nest. She doubted she'd sleep again, but she could try.

Fifteen minutes later, her growling stomach prodded her out of bed. She grabbed a banana from the kitchen, showered, dressed, and was out the door and on her way to meet with Tod for lunch before she had the chance to consider canceling and climbing back into bed with a good book. Tod wasn't going anywhere; there was no point in putting off the inevitable. She'd eat, commiserate, and run, and she could be back home and in jammies again before she knew it.

It was a perfect spring day: in just the few days since Verna's return, the temperatures had dropped, the trees had begun to bud, and the tempers of the pedestrians Winnie passed now had improved dramatically. Gone were the sweaty, angry commuters, the screaming children flush with prickly heat, the aggressive businessmen with ties pulled askew. Instead, everywhere Winnie looked, she saw content bystanders chatting into phones and drinking iced coffees and bouncing along to music only they could hear through wireless headphones. Even with the miserable lunch she was about to face, Winnie couldn't help but feel that, generally, all was right with the world again.

But when she pushed open the door of The Buttercup Café and spied Tod sitting alone at a small table looking out on the street, his long face pale and his black hair mussed and dirty, her buoyancy deflated.

"Hi, Tod," she said, sliding in across from him and laying her sunglasses on the table. "How was your night?" She regretted the question as soon as it had left her mouth; it was clear from his rumpled clothing that he had slept in them.

"I didn't know where to go last night after you kicked me out, so I just went home," he responded morosely. Winnie scowled. She could think of a better way to express being asked to leave someone's home after not having been invited there in the first place, but Tod wasn't looking at her, and she let the dig pass without comment. Tod gazed into his coffee. "I suppose Verna felt bad for me because she gave me a handful of cash and told me to find a hotel."

"Well, that's not so bad." Winnie tried to sound upbeat. It would have been unkind to point out that Tod may have slept in a hotel, but he still looked like he'd slept under a city bus. Did they not have running water where he'd stayed?

He moaned, "But she didn't send me with a toothbrush or a change of clothes!" He looked down at his tee-shirt as if he'd never seen it before, though Winnie certainly remembered it from the night before.

A suspicious spot near his collar prompted her to ask, "Did you order food? Why don't we do that first."

They ordered, Winnie requesting a Bloody Mary to fortify herself for the conversation that she anticipated would accompany the food.

When she had her drink and had taken a few energizing sips, she sat back in her chair. "Okay, Tod. Spill it. What's going on?"

Winnie wouldn't have thought it possible, but Tod's dour expression fell even farther. "I really love your sister, Winnie. I love her more than I know how to express. She loves me back, right?"

Whatever Winnie had been expecting, it hadn't been this. In the little bit of time she'd been able to steal for her own thoughts since she, Verna, and Tod had returned from the Depths, Winnie had struggled with her feelings about their relationship. Tod seemed to love Verna, and vice versa, but Winnie's stomach curdled a bit when she thought of how that love had come about. What kind of person kidnapped another person? How had that affected her sister? She was determined to accept the situation for what it was, trust Verna to make decisions for her own life, and respect those decisions, but the niggling doubts she had about Tod persisted.

"Well, I don't mean this to sound as...cruel as I suppose it does, but she caused a lot of problems just to be with you. I can't really imagine her doing that for someone she didn't care for." This must be true, although she hadn't thought of it that way until just that moment.

"I guess you're right. I mean, I hope you're right. After we left your dad's shop that night we came back, she was mad. Really mad. I thought she was mad at your folks or at Meri for spilling the beans about the baby, but she was mad at me!" He said this with a look of appeal that suggested Winnie ought to gasp with shocked horror at the suggestion.

Instead, she sipped her Bloody Mary placidly, studying Tod. He stared back earnestly, waiting for Winnie's response.

"Well," she finally answered diplomatically, "in Verna's defense, Meri, Mom, and Dad never kidnapped and imprisoned her. So, there's that."

Maybe Winnie was angrier than she'd liked to admit about the circumstances leading up to Verna and Tod's marriage. Now that she had Tod sitting humbled before her, she struggled to control the urge to kick him while he was down. Saying such a hurtful thing felt good in the moment, but as she watched Tod's face fall again, she regretted being so snappish. What happened to her determination to respect Verna's decisions and move forward? She sighed deeply. Maybe she was wrong about Tod. Maybe what she was really angry about was the stress of Verna's absence.

"Tod, that wasn't the kindest response I could have given you…"

"No," Tod cut her off before she could add a *but* to the end of her sentence. "You're right to be angry, Winnie. Your whole family is right to be angry. Even

Verna. I can't tell you how many times I've thought through what I did and cringed with regret."

Winnie threw caution to the wind. She had anticipated never having a decent response to her questions about Verna's disappearance, but Tod seemed to be in the mood to repent. She'd be a fool not to take advantage of it.

"Then why did you do it, Tod?" she prodded, leaning forward and attempting to catch his downturned eyes. "What made you ever think it was a good idea?"

It was Tod's turn to sigh. He was about to respond when the food came, and there was a brief tizzy of rearranging as the server set down plates and returned with extra napkins.

When they were once again alone, Winnie stared expectantly at Tod. "Go on. Let's hear it," she told him.

"I saw Verna when I was topside for a visit. I came up from time to time, just to see how the world was changing and to get a break from…you know…"

"All the dead people?" Winnie suggested.

"Yes." Tod took a bite of his sandwich and chewed without enthusiasm. Swallowing, he said, "I saw her in a bookstore. I liked having new books to keep me distracted from…well…"

Winnie made a *get on with it* gesture. They'd still be sitting here when the café closed if he continued at this rate. "Dead people. Got it."

"Anyway, I saw Verna, and she was so beautiful. So alive. And that was really appealing after being surrounded all the time by so many…um…"

"Mention dead people one more time, Tod, and I'll figure out a way for you to join them again," Winnie growled around a mouthful of tuna salad.

"Sorry." Tod stared balefully into his lap like a chastised child.

"So, Verna catches your eye…" Winnie prompted.

"You have to understand that before that day, I'd been unhappy for a long time. I hated being *down there*." He raised his eyebrows significantly, and Winnie began to wonder if he ever referred directly to his position as the death Fundamental. "I longed for freedom, but clearly that wasn't possible. But the more I thought about Verna, the more I wondered about the possibility of having a companion. I thought I could stand to be what I was if I didn't have to do it alone. And Verna seemed like the perfect being to fill that space."

Winnie screwed up her eyebrows in confusion. "Wait a minute. Did you know Verna was spring? When you took her?"

Winnie was amazed to see Tod somehow manage to look even more pathetic. "I might have followed her for several years."

Winnie dropped her fork with a clatter, the chunk of cantaloupe she'd just speared shooting off the side of her plate. "You didn't," she whispered, aghast.

"I know it was wrong—"

"Well, that makes me feel better!" she scoffed. "Does my sister know about this?" Winnie checked her volume, aware of the few other occupants in the tiny dining room.

"Yes!" Tod insisted, lowering his voice as well but still managing to sound pathetic. "I told her all of this, Winnie. When I released her, I made a clean breast of it. I confessed to following her and finding out her true nature, and I told her I thought I'd have to kill her—"

"What?" This time Winnie's voice cut through the susurration of conversation in the small establishment, and several neighboring patrons turned to look at her. She glanced around shamefacedly, waving little finger-waggles of apology at the adjacent onlookers.

"I thought she'd have to die to stay with me. I didn't know at the time whether or not she'd be able to stay with me as an Elemental since her season wouldn't happen without her. I figured the easiest solution was to kill her. Then she could stay with me."

Winnie's mouth hung open in disbelief, and Tod scrambled to explain further. "Winnie, I was in a terrible place. You have to understand that. I was desperate, and I wasn't thinking clearly at all. I would never have suggested such an awful thing if I weren't so miserable!"

Winnie huffed once and leaned back in her chair. She studied Tod in silence.

"Anyway," he went on after deciding she wasn't going to respond. "Once I had her...*there*...I found I couldn't bring myself to do what I thought I needed to do. I ended up just holding her there, fighting with myself and going over it again and again. Then one day, when I went to see her, she had made creeping thyme grow all over the floor of her cell. I thought it was a provocation: she'd been trying to lure me into talking to her for weeks. So, we talked. And I knew then that she'd be the right woman to be a partner to me. But I also began to realize that I could never kill her, even if nothing would make me happier than having her stay with me.

"After that night, I went back to talk to her every day. And she talked back. We just…got to know each other. Until finally, one day, I opened the cell."

"You gave her the chance to leave?" Winnie remembered the food on her plate and absently picked up half of her sandwich. She held it as if about to take a bite, but she never raised it to her mouth. She simply watched Tod, spellbound.

"I did. I realized I loved her. I loved her too much to keep her caged. And then I was disgusted at what I'd done. I was embarrassed that I'd ever acted so selfishly. I apologized, and I told her I would open a door for her if she wanted to leave."

"And what did she say?"

For the first time, Tod grinned, although it was a sad expression that might more accurately have been called a grimace. Tod's milky skin and slender, crooked nose contributed to the impression.

"She asked if she could stay a little longer. And that was it, Winnie. I gave her a room near mine, and we spent time together until finally…" He trailed off, and Winnie picked up the story.

"She married you."

"She did." Tod propped one elbow up on the table and rested his head in his hand. "And now she hates me." His words were distorted by the heel of his palm.

"I'm sure she doesn't hate you." Winnie had no idea why she was offering this consolation; for all she knew, Verna did indeed hate this man now that she was back in her old life and seeing the situation through her family's eyes. Frankly, Winnie wondered if hating Tod wasn't exactly what all of them should be doing. Her head began to spin.

But it was enough for Tod. "You don't think so?" he asked, a new glimmer in his eye. "I was hoping you'd say that, Winnie. It would mean a lot if you'd just tell her how much I love her."

Winnie held up her hands, her palms facing her brother-in-law. "Whoa, whoa, whoa. Slow down. I never said anything about talking to Verna on your behalf."

Tod pressed his lips into a thin line and held Winnie's gaze. "Umm…"

"Oh my god. Tell me you didn't, Tod."

"Hear me out, Winnie," Tod pleaded, reaching out to grasp Winnie's wrist.

But there was nothing to hear because at that moment, Winnie heard her name. She turned to see Verna standing in the café's entryway, her slender arms crossed over her chest and a thunderous look on her face.

Five

"Honey!" Tod exclaimed, shooting up out of his chair so suddenly that he jostled the table, and only Winnie's quick reflexes prevented her Bloody Mary from falling over. She righted the drink as Verna's shadow fell across the table, but when she looked up at her sister, she found that Verna wasn't looking at her but rather at her husband.

"Don't *honey* me," she hissed acerbically, and Tod dropped back into his chair with an audible *whump*. Winnie was sure she heard his teeth clack together. He gazed up at his wife balefully. Winnie had a strong urge to kick him hard in the shin, whether to break him forcibly out of his morose stupor or simply as a show of solidarity with her sister she couldn't say.

Verna had leaned down over the table and was whisper-screaming at Tod, working hard both to imbue her voice with scolding anger and to avoid the attention of diners at neighboring tables. Winnie could have told her she was wasting her time; occupants at several tables were openly spectating, apparently having decided the little table at the front of the café was going to continue to provide fresh entertainment throughout their meals.

"I can't believe you'd trick me into meeting you here like this! I told you I needed time to think about everything that happened! You should respect my wishes, Tod! Not lure me out on false pretenses..." Verna's gaze trawled the half-eaten dishes on the table. "And you clearly arranged this so that you two would be here first!" She turned angry eyes on Winnie. "Has he been trying to convince you to butter me up on his behalf, Winnie?"

Winnie had been sipping her drink, watching the drama unfold between her sister and brother-in-law, but at Verna's sudden inquisition, she tried to swallow and respond simultaneously and began coughing. Verna's brow furrowed in concern, and she reached behind Winnie to thump her on the back a few times. Tod took advantage of the diversion to grimace with contrition and shake his head at Winnie in vigorous entreaty. He pressed his palms together in prayer.

Please don't tell my wife I asked you to come here to talk to her on my behalf, his eyes screamed at Winnie.

"Tod asked me to come here to talk to you on his behalf," Winnie finally managed to splutter, and Tod's body slumped in on itself like a poorly constructed tent.

"Thanks a lot, Winnie," he said resignedly, clearly girding himself for what was to follow.

Verna, who had been studying Winnie as she first choked and then confessed, turned to face her husband with a deliberate slowness that made even Winnie's neck hair prickle with caution. But when Verna spoke, rather than continue to whisper-scream, she clearly and calmly addressed her husband. Each word was clipped and precise. Winnie's eyes widened in concern.

"Exactly what did you think would be the outcome of this little tête-à-tête-à-tête, Tod?"

"There aren't three têtes in that saying, honey. It's just tête-à-tête. It's French…for…," he trailed off, looking back and forth between his sister-in-law and his wife. Verna went still, and the climate around the intimate table seemed to crackle with the ozone of a coming storm.

Winnie stared at Tod, her mouth falling open and one hand rising slowly until her palm and her mouth met with perfect synchronicity. She watched what she suspected were Tod's last few moments of life through splayed fingers.

Tod swallowed so loudly that the man behind him scooted his chair forward a few inches to get out of the blast zone.

"What did you just say?" Verna asked icily. Her eyes had narrowed to slits. She continued to lean over the table, and Winnie could see that Verna's fingertips, splayed tensely on the tablecloth, had turned white.

"...head-to-head," Tod finished lamely.

Verna whacked him on the shoulder with her billfold. "I know what it means, Tod!" she snarled through clenched teeth as Tod rubbed his shoulder.

Just then, Winnie noticed their server push through the swinging kitchen door, and she seized the opportunity to prevent a very public homicide. Winnie had worked too hard to get her sister out of one captive situation to have her end up in a mortal jail.

"Oh, Verna, look! Here comes our server! Let's flag her down and order you some lunch. Are you hungry for lunch? I'm sure you're hungry. I mean, you're eating for two now, right? How about a Monte Cristo? You love a Monte Cristo. Isn't the Monte Cristo the lunch special today, Tod? Excuse me!" she trilled, spastically waving her fingers toward the server, a rail-thin woman of at least sixty whom Winnie feared likely didn't have the upper body strength to help her forcibly remove her sister's fingers from around her brother-in-law's neck.

The addition of the server to their trio seemed to defuse Verna. A chair was supplied within moments, and Verna sank into it stiffly yet willingly. Her eyes never left her husband's pale face.

When Verna's order had been taken and the server had nervously withdrawn, Winnie cleared her throat. "Verna, how are you feeling? No morning sickness or…anything?"

For a moment, Winnie thought her sister might completely ignore her and continue to stare at Tod in stony silence, but finally Verna turned her attention fully on her sister, her body following so that in the space of a moment, she was as engaged in pretending Tod wasn't there as she had been in focusing on nothing but him.

Winnie could feel Tod wilt from across the table, but she followed Verna's lead and ignored him completely. It was a little too easy to do, and as she half-listened to Verna's detailed report of the microscopic changes to her body over the last few days, she pondered the ease with which both of them cut Tod out of the conversation.

While it was true that a sizable part of her reveled in his exclusion and her own superior connection with Verna, a louder, more mature part of her cringed with concern. Verna and Tod's beginnings had been unusual, certainly, and it would take time for the Harvesters to adjust to their new family member, but all of the individuals in that equation were adults, beings of vast experience and (in some cases less vast) wisdom. The bumpy road that may lie before them all was navigable. But now Verna was pregnant; a new little being was going to enter the world, and that being had no tools for negotiating the pitfalls of tricky relationships. It would need the guidance of the adults in its life to know how to be a…Fundamental? Elemental? Something else entirely? Winnie couldn't even begin to think through the ramifications of this little creature's parentage, but she knew that, as its family, her responsibility was to set the best example she could. Was it right for her to be enjoying alienating her brother-in-law? After all, Tod was no longer simply her sister's husband. He was the father of Winnie's first niece or nephew.

When she considered the complicated feelings she held toward Tod through that filter, they suddenly seemed less complicated. Whether or not she trusted him—she did not—and whether or not she liked him— definitely no—she felt a strong pang of allegiance to the baby his addition to their lives had created.

She hadn't really been listening to her sister for the last several minutes, so she didn't hesitate to interrupt her. "Verna, I think you and Tod need to talk through whatever's going on here."

Verna, who had apparently been mid-sentence, stared at her in surprise. Tod sat upright, apparently as surprised by Winnie's suggestion as his wife.

Verna's mouth hardened into a line, but Winnie considered again the little sprout unfurling in her sister's belly and plunged ahead.

"You're right to be mad at Tod for asking you to come here and not telling you ahead of time that I was going to be here too. Deceit has no place in a marriage." She looked pointedly at her brother-in-law. "Tod, you shouldn't have tricked Verna—"

"But I didn't mean to—"

Winnie held up her hand to silence him. "Don't respond. You shouldn't have done it, and that's it. You'll have to apologize."

Beside Winnie, Verna turned to shoot Tod a triumphant smirk.

"And you'll need to apologize too," Winnie continued, raising her eyebrows at her sister's profile.

Verna spun to gawp at Winnie. "What do I have to apologize for?"

"For sending your husband away without any explanation, for one thing. If you really needed to be alone, that's fine. But you can't expect the person you married and then moved into a completely different world to simply figure out where to go and what to do when you can't be bothered with him."

"I didn't expect him to just figure it out! I gave him your key!" Verna raised her voice in indignation.

Winnie was used to her sister's excitability, and she had long ago learned that out-shouting Verna was an impossibility. So, she leaned back calmly and responded quietly, "Yes. Thank you for reminding me that I deserve an apology, too. It isn't my job to be available at all hours for family counseling."

Verna studied Winnie carefully. "You've changed, Winnie." Her tone wasn't critical; rather, Verna sounded almost reverential.

Winnie nodded. "I have. So have you. And I'd like to believe Tod has as well, or plans to, if the two of you are really going to overcome the very bad way this marriage started." Verna's cheeks flushed crimson.

Winnie looked at Tod in the silence that followed her proclamation. He held her gaze, but Winnie found that his expression betrayed neither indignation nor shame. She was struck momentarily by how very like his own anchor pools Tod's black eyes were: what might one see in their depths? She wasn't sure she wanted to know the answer to that.

Breaking the silence, she said, "My point, you two, is that whatever's going on can't be worse or, frankly, weirder than what you've already gone through. So, what's the problem?"

Verna threw up her hands. "Oh, Winnie! I had no idea how hard it would be to come back! I mean, I knew it would be hard: I knew Mom and Dad were going to be furious, and I knew I'd have a lot of explaining to do, but I didn't realize how hard it was going to be to convince them that we did the right thing! And when everyone questions your decisions, it's hard to know if…you know…"

Tod's voice cut across her, stinging and frigid. "I knew it. I knew you were regretting marrying me."

Verna glanced at him but said nothing. Instead, she slumped as well. Winnie looked from one to the other of them; then, she folded her napkin, set it on the table beside her plate, and sat forward.

"Suck it up."

Two sets of eyes were suddenly riveted on Winnie, and she took advantage of the rapt attention.

"Both of you, just suck it up. You're adults. Tod, you made a dumb move kidnapping my sister. I get that you think you had a good reason, but you might as well hear it from me that just because you have an explanation, it doesn't mean any of us has to accept it.

"Verna, I'm not in a position to judge you for agreeing to marry Tod—that whole situation is complicated beyond my ability to comprehend. But you caused a lot of trouble by not being forthright with your family as soon as you could have been. You should have been here managing your season. At the very least, you should have let us know you were okay. Not doing that caused a lot of worry and a lot of problems, and you're going to have to figure those out with everyone who still has hard feelings."

Verna and Tod sat staring at Winnie, their eyes large and unblinking. Winnie felt compelled to say one more thing, and she plunged ahead.

"Mom and Dad will get used to the situation. So will Meri and Autumn. And me too, for that matter. But when it's all said and done, it really makes no difference who gets used to what. Verna, it doesn't matter that you're having a judgment crisis. Tod, it also doesn't matter that you're feeling sorry for yourself.

The two of you made a bed together, literally. And in that bed, you made a baby. Swallow your egos, make your peace, and apologize to the people you owe apologies to. You've both made terrible decisions; endeavor to make better decisions together for yourselves and your baby from here on out. Got it?"

Verna nodded obediently, and Tod croaked out an affirmation around his convulsing Adam's apple.

Winnie stood. "Good," she pronounced. "I don't want to hear from either one of you until you've got this sorted out."

With that, Winnie clutched her purse, turned, and strode out of the restaurant. It wasn't until she was three blocks away that she realized with satisfaction that she'd left Verna and Tod with the check.

Six

For three days after the confrontation at the café, Winnie didn't hear from anyone. Pete didn't call her to ask if she could help him tidy up the office at the rock shop, Brooke didn't call to vent about Verna's disrespectful behavior (not that she'd been likely to; she and Winnie hadn't properly spoken since they'd had unpleasant words before Verna's return), Autumn didn't call to complain about her seasonal allergies since spring had finally arrived, and Meri hadn't called to gush over Annabella, her latest love interest.

And the silence had been delightful.

Winnie had stayed up late every night, reading in bed with a bowl of ice cream and a glass of wine. Then she'd slept late each morning, lounging in her blanket nest until her stomach began to growl. Then she'd putter around her kitchen, chatting absently with Nina through a shallow water dish on her counter and flipping pancakes as she sipped coffee. She didn't even scold herself when half the batter sat out too long and had to be thrown away.

So it came as a change of pace when, on the fourth day after walking out of her lunch with Tod, she received a phone call from, of all people, Verna. She looked at the face of her ringing phone before answering, considering just for that moment rejecting the call. She was halfway through a good book, and golden sunlight was suffusing her little balcony with perfect reading light. Her thumb hovered over the decline icon before swinging over to tap the answer icon instead. She may regret it today, but she was going to have to talk to her sister sooner or later.

"Hiya, sis," she said into the phone.

"Hi, Winnie," Verna responded, the typical burble of her voice subdued. "I'm calling to apologize."

Winnie sat down at her kitchen table. Verna was proud; this could take a while.

"I'm listening," she said.

It didn't take as long as Winnie expected. In fact, it was one of the shortest apologies Winnie had ever received, and she grinned in appreciation when she ended the call minutes later. Verna had simply owned up: she'd done the wrong thing. She'd made bad decisions. And she'd ended up hurting people she loved. For all of those things, she was sorry. She and Tod had talked through their troubles, and they were both going to be working over the next few months to make right everything that had gone wrong so that they were ready to welcome their new baby into a happy, loving home. Winnie had accepted her sister's apology with grace, asking only that Verna reach out to her with any request for help. Verna promised to do so and rang off to place several more calls. Winnie didn't have to ask who she was calling to know that all of the Harvesters would be receiving calls.

Settling herself on the balcony in a low chaise, Winnie sighed. She'd been worried, although she had spent almost no time in the last few days hashing over the fight in the café. Some part of her, though, had been tense about the conflict with Verna and Tod, perhaps even a bit tense on their behalf as well, worried about how they'd make peace with Pete and Brooke. And though she hadn't spoken to any of her family members and therefore had no way of guessing, she wondered if any of them could ever learn to trust Tod.

But Verna clearly had given the situation a great deal of thought; Winnie was confident that, one way or another, everything was going to turn out just fine.

Probably.

After her sister's absence of more than a year, Winnie might have suspected the Harvester sisters' old routines would take time to get reestablished. They had always been close siblings, and they'd formed patterns that had become habits of years, even decades, but Verna's disappearance had been a major disruption. Yet as the days after Verna and Tod's reconciliation turned into weeks, Winnie began to feel as though little had changed after all. The girls picked up their weekly lunch date at the café, and as they settled into their old groove, their conversations turned more and more to Verna's growing belly and the changes her new baby would bring.

The four Harvester sisters were Pete and Brooke's only children, and they represented—as far as they knew—a generation all their own. There were other beings out there like them, of course: Tod was a Fundamental, a being whose power over death maintained the balance of mortal lives. There were other Fundamentals, but their lives and the forces they controlled were entirely separate from Winnie and her Elemental family. The Fundamentals concerned themselves with the daily doings of the mortal beings that inhabited the world they all shared, and the Elementals managed the larger forces that made the world around those mortals habitable.

Winnie and her sisters knew, too, that there were other Elementals besides themselves, but Pete and Brooke had kept even those more immediate family members out of the girls' lives. Winnie, Autumn, Meri, and Verna had never questioned that decision. The four of them had each other, and the girls had their parents, and if Brooke and Pete had dealings with those other Elementals, they didn't discuss it with the girls.

Winnie had never questioned this state of affairs. She and her sisters managed the seasons handily. Brooke and Pete, whose concerns were vaster but less cyclical—Brooke's element was water and Pete's was earth—didn't talk with the girls about those elements' demands. Abstractly, Winnie supposed there must be other Elementals and Fundamentals out there managing the many functions that ensured human life continued, but she'd never had reason to investigate that supposition.

But that insularity, like Verna's expanding body, was changing. Had a Fundamental and an Elemental ever produced a child together? The Harvester girls couldn't answer that question. And while they had their self-contained, little family, Tod seemed to have no one at all. Yet, he must have come from somewhere. Who were his parents? Where were they? And did he have siblings? What did they make of this strange coupling and the baby that was on the way?

At one of their weekly lunches, mid-summer, when Meri had taken over local temperate duties and Verna was able to relax and allow her other seasonal regions to chug along without much intervention, Autumn asked that very question. Did Tod have family? And if he did, where were they?

Verna sat back in her chair, her hand clutched protectively over the mound of napkin-draped midsection that filled the space between her and the table. She'd hardly touched her salmon, asserting that the new pressure in her midsection made her appetite bigger but the actual volume of food she could consume smaller.

"I don't really know," she said distractedly, sipping lemon water through a straw. It was clear from the look on her face that she was reviewing past conversations in her mind. "I've asked him about his family a few times, but he gets kind of…funny when I do."

"Ooh, funny how?" Meri asked, leaning forward at the suggestion of gossip. "Do you think he's hiding something?"

Verna didn't answer immediately, and Winnie furrowed her brow, suddenly suspicious.

"Verna?" she prompted. Verna's head snapped up to look at her, her eyes searching Winnie's as if she'd been caught doing something she shouldn't have been.

"No!" She said it too loudly, and all three sisters paused to study Verna's face. She laughed with embarrassment and looked from one sister to the next without finding a sympathetic chuckle on any of the women's faces.

"Spill," Autumn snapped, her owlish gaze commanding Verna's attention.

"Spill what?" Verna countered. Her tone was light, but the Harvester sisters had been in the sibling business longer than most other beings on Earth; they weren't fooled by her subterfuge.

Meri reached across the table, grasping Verna's hand. "Vee," she said in her *abiding patience* voice. "If something is going on that you're concerned about, you can share that with us. You know we're your safe place."

Winnie swallowed an impulse to roll her eyes, and Autumn scoffed. "Don't think the same protection extends to your husband, though," she added.

Meri shot her a scornful look, but Winnie was secretly pleased to discover that even after weeks of getting to know Tod, Autumn still hadn't forgiven the complicated beginning of his relationship with Verna either.

"You're overreacting," Verna insisted, pulling her hand out of Meri's and picking again at her fish. Winnie knew that trick; she tapped Meri's shin with her toe when it seemed like Meri might start talking just to fill the silence. When Meri looked her way, Winnie shook her head just the slightest bit. Verna wasn't going to eat her way out of answering their questions.

The four sat in silence as Verna ate with unnatural focus. Meri, Autumn, and Winnie watched her patiently, unspeaking. Just when it seemed Meri might burst from the oppressive silence, Verna glanced up from her food into three expectant faces.

Her shoulders sagged, and she released her fork with a *clack* against the rim of the plate.

"Okay, fine. I give up." She sighed and leaned back in her chair, dropping her napkin onto her plate. "I've asked Tod about his family a few times, and he gets kind of defensive about it. It's not like he's hiding anything," she added pointedly, tipping her head toward Autumn. "I'm not saying it's suspicious or that I'm concerned about it. I'm just saying that when I bring it up, it's clear that he doesn't want to discuss any of that stuff."

"And you really don't find that suspicious?" Autumn prompted, and Winnie knew the measure of Autumn's self-control. She would normally have been derisive, but just this once she seemed to be modulating her response carefully. Autumn pretended aloofness, but Winnie suspected she was as excited about the tiny newcomer Verna carried as her sisters were and was loath to jeopardize her goodwill with Verna.

"No, I really don't," Verna responded. "Well…" she amended, "not very. I mean if any of us had to describe our relationships with one another to an outsider, that would be really difficult, right?"

Winnie thought back a few months to the day she had sat in her mother's formal front room with Nina after having spent hours trying to describe Brooke to her new friend. It had indeed been tricky.

"So, if he has a weird relationship with his family, it's not totally unexpected that he wouldn't want to try to explain it to me."

Winnie looked at Autumn, who had turned her way with one eyebrow cocked. Neither of them glanced toward Meri, who almost certainly would agree with Verna's assessment. But then Meri had once tried to adopt a possum she'd found in an alley, so her sisters tended to throw out her vote when they debated whether or not something sounded sensible.

"That wouldn't be unexpected if he was asked to explain it to one of us," Autumn informed Verna. "But you're his *wife*. If he can't have a difficult conversation with you, who can he have one with?"

Verna looked down at her napkin-covered plate and didn't answer. A wave of unease washed over Winnie, and she wished suddenly and strongly that they were talking about anything but this topic. She pushed down the feeling. Verna was home, and in a few months, the Harvester family would expand for the first time in many mortal lifetimes.

Concerning or not, Tod wasn't going anywhere.

Seven

By the time summer faded into fall and Autumn began the process of putting great swathes of the Northern Hemisphere to sleep, Verna's belly had swelled to the size of the cheery, orange pumpkin that sat atop Winnie's stoop. The snap of impending cold now crept through Winnie's open windows in the evenings once the sun went down, and as she did each fall, she relished the chilly morning air that greeted her when she woke, swaddled up to her eyes in her toasty down blanket.

She spent more time at home now that night was coming earlier, and as a result, she spent more of her evenings visiting with Nina and, when he was in the mood, Abel. Tod's departure had changed Abel; perhaps a stranger wouldn't notice his occasional joke or how patient he was with Nina's lighthearted but often constant chattering, but Winnie had known the old, indentured Abel, and this freer, more tolerant version was a notable improvement.

One night, after her calls to Nina had become her favorite weekly routine, Winnie had been astonished when a story she related about a pushy solicitor her mother had run off with a bizarrely persistent and extraordinarily localized cloudburst drew a bark of laughter from Abel. Winnie had gaped at his watery image in her dish of anchor water, but Nina laughed along with him as if the raucousness were perfectly normal. Perhaps, Winnie reflected after the call, it was. Nina had settled into her new job, and Abel had settled right along beside her, and Winnie was pleased for both of them. He still wouldn't be Winnie's first choice for company on a Friday night, but the camaraderie between Nina and him was apparent; Winnie would never tell Abel as much, but she was thankful that Nina had him as both a colleague and a companion.

Occasionally, she'd receive a text from Nolan, usually asking her to pass along a message to his sister. Winnie had walked Nolan through the process of contacting Nina, and she knew from their conversations that Nina reached out to him often, but Nolan hadn't quite gotten comfortable with the idea of teleconferencing with the afterlife. Secretly, Winnie didn't mind this discomfort: she didn't mention it to Nina, but each time Nolan's name appeared on her phone's screen, she felt a thrill of excitement. It was nothing serious, certainly. Nothing meaningful. But she neglected to mention it to Nina nonetheless and spent no time at all wondering why that might be.

It was on one of these enjoyable evenings with Nina that the call came. She was sitting in the cozy armchair in her front room where she normally sat with her anchor dish, gazing down into the water and working her way gradually through a bottle of Malbec. Nina was doing her best to explain something that Winnie found utterly incomprehensible.

"So, the wraith came back to me for a third time, this poor newbie trailing behind him, saying he'd taken her to the exact spot her father should be *again*, and they still hadn't found him. I was certain, Winnie, that I'd sent him to the right place. This guy was already, you know, wraithing or whatever when I took over here, so I freaked out a little. I mean, he's the expert, and he's coming to me to figure out a problem? Yikes."

"I guess that's the sucky part of being the boss, then? The problems tend to trickle up to you?"

Nina rolled her eyes in agreement, but Winnie could see the rosy glow of pride on her cheeks. Whatever direction the story was heading so far, she knew Nina had figured it out in the end. She sipped her wine again, enjoying listening to her friend's narration.

"You bet they do. So, there I was trying to figure out what I was doing wrong or what he was doing wrong, and trying really hard not to look incompetent in front of this new essence who was probably getting pretty nervous that being dead might be like one long Terry Gilliam movie or something when Abel popped his head in."

"Abel to the rescue!" Winnie crowed. "What did he say?"

"Oh, Winnie, you won't believe it! He said 'did you try looking down?'"

"Down?" Winnie pondered this. "Down where?"

"That's what I said! You know Abel: he was delighted that he'd suddenly become the savior of the day. He took the assignment from the wraith, and off we went, searching for the same essence for a fourth time.

"When we finally got to the right place, it was just like the wraith had said: totally barren. Literally, Winnie, it was the middle of a prairie that spread out in every direction as far as the eye could see."

Winnie and Nina had spent some time together in the Depths where Nina was now running the show, so Winnie knew exactly what she meant by this. It wasn't an exaggeration: the landscape in the afterlife was malleable, appearing differently to different people and prone to mutation when one's back was turned. To spin on the spot in the middle of a field and see nothing but grass didn't mean that there wasn't a forest or a lake or a desert or even a skyscraper right behind you; it just meant it wasn't there *at the moment.* Winnie tried not to think about this too hard.

"So here we all are staring at, like, grass, and Abel says, 'here we are.' Now the wraith is looking at me like I should be doing something, and the newbie is looking at Abel like she can't decide whether he's pranking her or is just a genuine lunatic when Abel drops to his hands and knees and starts crawling around on the ground."

Winnie snorted. "What? What in the world?"

Nina's brown eyes twinkled excitedly. "I know! It was bananas! All of a sudden, Abel stops, looks at the name on the assignment, puts his face right by the ground, and yells 'Halloo, Martin!'"

"Into the ground?"

"Right…into…the ground." Nina put her hand up to swear, punctuating her statement with little nods that made her hair fall over her eyes. She swept it to the side absentmindedly. "I thought he'd lost his mind. But…" Nina sat forward, and Winnie did the same, as if a few inches of space would help bridge the dimensional divide between them.

"As we're all standing there watching this with our mouths hanging open, Abel reaches out to pick up something and turns to us...," Nina paused to draw out the big reveal, and Winnie felt herself starting to grin. "With a mouse."

Winnie's grin melted. She stared at Nina in puzzlement. "Come again?"

Nina had clearly been expecting this reaction, and she hooted with delight. "He was a mouse, Winnie! The soul we were looking for was a mouse! That's why the wraith couldn't find him. Abel found his little burrow and called to him, and out he came!"

Winnie sat back, processing his revelation. "You're telling me her father was a mouse?"

"Yes! Oh..." She tilted her head thoughtfully. "Well, no. Of course he wasn't a mouse. That wouldn't make any sense."

"*That's* what wouldn't make sense?" Winnie gaped at her friend.

Nina giggled, tipping a little more wine into her glass.

"Her father was a human when he was alive, of course. He wasn't a mouse then. But for whatever reason, when he died, the afterlife he imagined for himself was as a rodent."

Winnie didn't say anything for a moment. "That's a thing?" she finally asked. "People can be animals?"

"Yep. Abel says it's pretty rare, so many wraiths never encounter one before they move on. But he's been here so long that he knows all about them. Isn't that nuts?"

"Completely," Winnie agreed, marveling at the realities of the world around her that still surprised her. She'd been alive for so long that it had become easy to feel as though she knew all there was to know. But the last year had certainly shown her how wrong she was: life was full of the unknown, even for her.

Hard on that thought came another. "Tod should have told you that, Nina," she said critically. "He should have prepared you better."

Nina waved a dismissive hand. "That was such a crazy time. Some things were sure to fall through the cracks."

Winnie scoffed. "People turning into animals seems like a pretty big thing to fall through a crack. How long would it have taken him to mention? 'By the way,'" Winnie intoned, adopting her best Tod voice, "'don't swat a mosquito. It could be someone's Uncle Edward.'"

Nina giggled again, but Winnie could see that she wasn't convinced. "You're too hard on him, Winnie. He left Abel here with me for exactly that reason, remember? This place has so many moving parts, there's no way he could have gotten me completely comfortable before leaving."

"I think you're more forgiving than I am, Nina."

Nina smiled kindly. "Only because it wasn't my family he disrupted. I'm not saying you don't have the right to be angry with him still. It doesn't seem that way, does it? I only mean that being angry won't make you feel better about the situation."

Winnie, who had felt her blood beginning to warm, smiled back at her friend. As always, Nina was right. Tod would never be her favorite person, but it wasn't doing her any good to look for reasons to be madder at him than she already was.

The chirping of her phone interrupted these thoughts. She glanced at the screen and swallowed.

"Speaking of disrupting the family...," she said as she leaned over to pick the phone, which had stopped trilling for only a moment before starting up again. "Guess what time it is, Nina?"

Nina's eyes grew big. "Oh my gosh! Tell Verna and Tod congrats from me!"

Winnie had already grabbed her bag and jammed her feet into topsiders. Her joyful shout to Nina was cut short by the slamming of her front door.

Eight

Across the world, in a filthy apartment, a hulking mass of unkempt man gazed with furrowed brow at the televisions arrayed before him. It was mid-morning, but heavy, cobwebbed drapes obscured the meager daylight that might have illuminated the room with natural light. As it was, the room was indeed lit, but it was suffused with the fatiguing, flickering light of the dozen or so screens that ran constantly, scrolling image after image of unrest and discord around the world.

Damion Strife took it all in. His broad form never moved; from the other side of the filthy room, where a shaking lackey now swiped at the sweat prickling his forehead under the band of his baseball cap, Strife seemed eerily still but for the haze of flies buzzing around his head. Had the lackey stepped around the piles of stinking food containers on the floor and moved to look into the face of the man to whom he reported, however, he would have seen movement: Strife's eyes darted from screen to screen, never resting more than a few moments. Nothing he saw there elicited a reaction from the bear of a man.

But the lackey didn't dare move around to face his master. He had already stood there trembling for a quarter of an hour; the monster glued to the screens, though aware of his presence, still hadn't turned to receive the news the young man waited anxiously to deliver.

Suddenly, Strife moved, his body coming to life with pops and cracks that raised goosebumps on the messenger's arms. When Strife spun to face him, the boy choked out a ragged breath, his eyes dropping instantly from Strife's face to the floor at his feet, where a swarm of fat, white maggots made steady work of what must once have been uneaten leftovers.

His gorge rose, and he closed his eyes.

"Speak," Strife said at last. His voice creaked like his body had, an aged thing long unused and reluctant to flex and contract.

The boy swallowed several times, afraid of his punishment if he vomited on the boss's floor.

"Err…sir," he managed to choke out, willing himself to look Strife in the face. Nothing could be worse than staring at the roiling maggots, surely.

But he was mistaken. Gazing at Strife, unspeaking, he wished he were still looking at the rotting meat on the floor.

"Well?" Strife growled, his black eyes unblinking.

"I'm supposed to tell you it's time," the boy croaked. "It's coming today." The boy didn't know what *it* was, what any of this message meant. And he didn't much care at the moment. He wanted only to leave this place, as quickly as possible.

"Go."

The boy didn't wait. He turned and fled, neglecting even to close the apartment door behind himself.

Strife stared after the boy, studying the open door. Then, he picked up the phone by his side and tapped the screen without looking at it.

It rang once before connecting, though no voice answered. Strife raised the phone to his ear and spoke.

"We need to talk."

"I told you I'd reach out to you when the time was right." The voice that responded was cold but powerful, its timbre fading to nothing in the putrid air of Strife's room. He drew the phone back from his ear a fraction of an inch.

"I won't wait much longer," came his reply. When the voice on the other end didn't respond, he spoke again. "We'll talk soon."

Nine

Renata Harvester, age three and a half, was fast asleep when Winnie showed up to babysit: her pouty pink lips were smashed against the frolicking-elephant print of her bedsheet, and her diapered derriere, propped skyward on two chubby, curled legs, was the first sight to greet her aunt when Winnie peeked into her room. Winnie snorted at the sight of her rumpled, mashed niece and turned to her sister, who was peering at her daughter over Winnie's shoulder, grinning dopily.

"What did you do, Verna, snip her strings?"

Verna snickered and raised her brows. Winnie was right: Renata did look a bit like a disused marionette.

"She always sleeps like that," Verna replied. She twisted at the waist to pop her spine. "Makes my back hurt just to look at her."

Verna smiled and pulled her little sister—nearly a head shorter than she—into a hug. Since the birth of the only Harvester baby in many, many years, Verna's body had gradually returned to its pre-baby shape. Mostly. It made Winnie secretly joyful to see her sister's rounder curves and softer features. As the rounder, softer sibling, Winnie had always cursed her sister's ease in wearing clothes off the rack; Winnie needed practically everything taken up or in, a consequence of having the bust, hip, and leg measurements suitable for three different sizes of clothing. But seeing Verna's blurred edges made Winnie appreciate her own measurements a little more.

Verna's fuller curves made her even more beautiful to her sister, though there had never been a time before Ren when she hadn't seemed perfectly lovely.

"What time is your reservation?" Winnie asked as she pulled away from Verna's embrace.

"Eight forty-five," Verna answered, looking at her watch. "Which means we have to run. Tod!" She turned to holler down the hallway, and Winnie hastily pulled Ren's door closed. "You have what you need, right, Winnie?" she asked as she strode away, not waiting for Winnie's response.

Winnie did have what she needed, which is to say she had a full knowledge of how to work Verna's remote and full access to the wine fridge. Ren wasn't likely to awaken before sunrise, and Winnie would snooze on the couch until her sister and brother-in-law returned to cover her with a blanket and tiptoe off to their bedroom. Then Winnie would join the little family for breakfast and spend the day with her snuggle-bug Ren, doting on the sweet, smiling baby. In the year since Renata's birth, this had become, more or less, her regular Friday night routine. Saturday nights she still reserved for calls with Nina.

But Renata broke the routine this Friday night. Winnie had just started to doze a couple of hours later when the sound of whimpering roused her. She pushed herself off the couch and muted the TV, setting her wineglass down on the kitchen counter and grabbing a sippy cup of ice water from the fridge before slipping quietly into Ren's room.

Renata sat up in her miniature bed, one sad pigtail drooping over her right ear and her face puckered with concern. When she saw Winnie, she reached out a pudgy, grasping hand and mewled pathetically.

"Annie Woo?"

"Hi, snuggle-bug," Winnie whispered as she lowered herself onto the side of the small bed. "How come you're up?" Ren climbed into Winnie's lap, plucking the sippy cup from her aunt's hand and settling into the same position she'd always slipped into when she still took a bottle. Winnie cuddled the girl against her torso, pulling both legs against her ribs on one side and cradling Ren's head in the crook of her opposite arm. She dug into the blankets until she came up with Butter Bear, Ren's much-loved and frequently laundered teddy bear. The velvet had rubbed off his nose and Brooke had needed to mend several of his seams, but Ren loved him as if he were in perfect condition. Winnie tucked the lumpy bear in against Ren's body, and the little girl raised her crooked elbow to let Winnie slide him into her embrace.

Renata was warm, and Winnie buried her face in the girl's neck, breathing in the sweet baby smells of sleep and heat and shampoo that Ren hadn't yet grown out of.

Winnie swayed slowly back and forward, rocking the toddler gently as they studied one another. Winnie smiled. She knew her heart couldn't really swell in response to the roly-poly little person in her arms, but in these quiet moments, that's exactly what she felt: her chest tightened, and her throat closed, and she felt so overcome by the reality of Renata that it felt like inflammation. She joked about nibbling on Ren's tiny fingers and toes, but while she was only teasing when she said it, the truth was that she could think of no other way to give voice to the feelings Ren evoked in her. Looking down into Ren's bright eyes now, she was so struck by the absolute faith this person had in her that she wanted to consume her, to gobble her up and hold the little form inside of her so that she'd always know her niece was safe and cared for. Winnie swallowed hard and cooed to the little girl, and Renata, calm and attentive, pulled the cup away from her face to grin up at Winnie.

Renata was really too big to be rocked the way Winnie rocked her now. Feeling the strain of holding her niece as an ache in her lower back, Winnie rose and shuffled backward until the seat of the glider in the corner of the room bumped the backs of her legs. Then, she settled down with Renata still spread across her. Ren's bright attention began to wane as Winnie rocked them both, and Winnie too could feel the soporific effect of the motion, the darkened bedroom, and the shushing sound machine. She rested her head on the back of the glider, tilting it at an awkward angle so that she could still look down into Ren's face even though the girl's eyes were starting to glaze over. It would be only a matter of minutes before she was back to sleep. It might be only a matter of minutes before Winnie was asleep as well.

Winnie reflected on the years that had passed since Renata's birth. The night she'd been born had felt momentous, not simply because there was a new member in the family, but because the bonds that had connected her family members to one another had felt suddenly renewed. In Verna's hospital room late that night, while the still-unnamed infant was still just a pink face buried somewhere inside a footprinted hospital blanket, the family had gathered to welcome her.

Winnie, who had been sitting back against the wall to give the new family space, had marveled at the tableau before her. Her parents, Pete and Brooke, stood to one side of Verna's bed, Pete's hands on Brooke's shoulder as he towered like a monolith behind his wife. It seemed unthinkable that the two of them could have been separated, so warm was the language of her mother's liquid form leaning back against her husband's powerful expanse. On the other side of the bed, Meri stood beside Tod, patting him affectionately on the back and jabbering about the plans she had for baby: teaching her to garden, collecting shells at the beach, explaining the rules of baseball, giving her dating advice...

Tod had been nodding, the line of irritation that only Meri seemed to be able to produce between his eyes gone for once, his pale face turned toward his wife and daughter. He leaned over them, one hand resting on Verna's shoulder, and the other daintily stroking his sleeping daughter's cheek. He had clearly been absorbed by her, smitten as they all were by her delicate eyelashes and miniature fingernails.

What does he see when he looks at her tiny face? Winnie had wondered. *What potential does he recognize in this little lady? And what power will she have? Containing the dead, like her father? Or planting the seeds of life, like her mother?*

Verna had glanced up at Tod, her eyes drowsy from the long day's work of bringing their tiny creation into the world but her aura serene: months of worry and anticipation were behind her now, and she held the fulfillment of their promise safely in her arms.

Autumn had come through the door at that moment with a pitcher of ice water from the nurses' station and, after filling Verna's thermal mug with fresh water, had taken her place beside Pete and Brooke. She'd slipped her hand into her mother's, and Brooke had turned to smile warmly at her coolest daughter, a smile Autumn returned.

Winnie had sat watching this from a remove, and she'd had the thought that this moment would be a photo in her mind: she'd recall this like a snapshot, the moment when all the people in her life had been gathered in perfect harmony, and for a fleeting instant, that idea made her melancholic, as if the photographic quality of it was provoked not by the joy of seeing all of these people together but by the unbearable transience of their solidarity.

Before Winnie could consider this feeling too deeply, Verna had broken in on Meri's incessant chatter.

"Renata," she'd proclaimed, her voice croaky but calm. Meri's mouth had snapped shut, and Brooke had reached out to push the blanket father back from the baby's face.

"Is that what you've decided to call her, then?" Brooke asked in uncharacteristically tender tones.

"It wasn't really a decision." Verna peered down into the face of her sleeping daughter. "I didn't know what to call her until just this minute. It just…came to me. And now that I've thought it, I can't really imagine calling her anything else."

"That's what happened to your mom when you girls were born," Pete interjected with a wistful smile.

Brooke tipped her head thoughtfully. "I wonder…," she murmured, but before Winnie had the chance to prod her to finish her question, she'd run her fingertips along the baby's brow and whispered, "Renata you are meant to be, and so you're called Renata."

Renata, Winnie thought now as she studied the sweet face of her sleeping niece. *Renata you are meant to be…*

Gingerly, Winnie rose, planting a row of soft kisses on Ren's brow; then, she lowered the girl into the crib. Ren arched and flailed momentarily before pulling Butter Bear against her chest, turning onto her belly, and tucking her legs under herself. Winnie grinned and patted the girl's elevated rump before picking up the empty cup and heading for the door.

She turned once in the doorway, the hallway light illuminating a last glimpse of the bed.

"Auntie Woo loves you, Ren," she whispered into the dark and pulled the door closed behind her.

Winnie was in the middle of a very strange dream when she was awakened. In it, she and Renata were stranded in the complicated, gnarled branches of a spreading elm, the sawtooth edges of the leaves whipping against their bare faces as the wind raged around them. How had they gotten up in this tree? Winnie's thoughts swirled with the wind around them. Ren was hardly big enough to get herself up into a kitchen chair; how had she managed to climb the tree? How was she holding so firmly to the branches?

Winnie looked down, her dream stomach lurching at the receding ground, but as she tore her gaze away to search for Ren again, she discovered that the great, rough-barked trunk had split into two powerful arms: somehow, she'd become stranded in the branching expanse of one arm, and Ren, clutching silently and wide-eyed to a swaying limb with her chubby arms and legs, had made her way up the other arm.

Winnie gulped, gaping at the distance between them. The tree must surely have grown larger in the few moments she'd been taking in her surroundings, for it seemed Ren was even farther away from her now.

Ren! she yelled. *Renata! Hold on! I'll come for you!*

But even as she yelled, Winnie could see that the tree was continuing to grow: the branch Ren clutched moved faster and faster, carrying the girl farther away.

Winnie looked down, desperate to find a safe place for her niece to land if she should fall, but the foot of the tree was lost in darkness, a black void so deep that it made her head spin to look at it.

She looked back at Renata, whose branch had taken her even higher and farther from her aunt's reach. Winnie squinted against the brightness of the sky behind her niece, a pure, white light that made her eyes ache. Its brightness felt caustic after the gaping blackness of what lay beneath them.

The wind gusted, shaking Winnie faster than ever, faster than any wind could possibly move. Winnie squeezed her eyes closed, fighting to hold on to the branch that vibrated back and forth beneath her. No wind could shake a tree like this.

Winnie! She heard a voice calling her, but when she opened her eyes to search out Ren—though the voice seemed too old and somehow familiar to belong to her—Winnie saw that her niece was just a flash of color in the distance, her purple pajamas visible only occasionally through the dense leaves of the canopy.

Winnie! the voice called again…and the shaking…

"Winnie! Wake up!"

Winnie's eyes flew open, and she clutched at the hand squeezing her biceps, shaking her almost painfully now.

"I'm awake," she growled, sleep clutching tenaciously at her eyes and throat. She pushed herself upright, disentangling herself from the blanket with sweaty, uncoordinated hands. "Verna?" She looked up into her sister's face, and the cloud of sleep and dream-branches dropped away so suddenly that Winnie felt a jolt of vertigo. "What's wrong?"

Verna's brows furrowed and her mouth contorted. "Winnie, what's going on? Where's Ren?"

Winnie drew back, uncomprehending. "Wh-what do you mean?" she stammered.

Tod's pale face had never looked so dark to Winnie as he pushed his wife aside and grabbed his sister-in-law's wrist.

"Renata isn't in her room, Winnie. She isn't here at all. You're the one who's supposed to be watching her. Where is our daughter?"

Ten

Winnie stared at Tod in uncomprehending horror.

Not in her room? Where else could she possibly be?

Her thoughts reeled, and for one sickening second, the vision of the wind-tossed elm from her dream forced out any rational thoughts that might have been trying to form there.

With effort, she cleared them from her mind and yanked her wrist from her brother-in-law's now-painful grip.

"That's ridiculous. She's here somewhere," she insisted, brushing past Verna as she marched down the hall to Ren's bedroom. "Where else could she be?" she called back over her shoulder. "It's not as if someone—"

She stopped dead, frozen by the sudden fear of what the end of that sentence might be.

It's not as if someone what? she thought. *Took her? Came into this apartment and snatched her away in the night?*

In a rage, she spun to face Tod. Ancient energy swirled in the air between them, and though Winnie had never produced a hot element in her life, the heat that built within her as she glared at the erstwhile master of death would have made hot-weather Meri proud.

"Where is Ren, Tod?" The voice that slithered from Winnie's mouth was hard and cold, so uncharacteristically Winnie that Verna reared back in shock.

Tod's pale face colored only slightly, but his mouth tightened into a firm, white line. "What makes you think I'd know that?" His lips scarcely parted as he responded.

Winnie took one step forward, raising her chin fractionally to keep her gaze locked on her brother-in-law. "Well, only one of us standing here has any experience with abducting someone from their bed in the middle of the night."

Tod fell back with a cry, throwing an arm out to steady himself against his wife. His mouth worked as if he might speak, but it was Verna's voice that broke Winnie's stare.

"What are you saying?" Her voice cracked, and Winnie studied her sister's face, trying to judge if it was shock or pain or fear that made her sound so small. Or possibly…anger.

"I'm just saying—"

"Saying what, exactly?" Tod cut in. "That I abducted my own daughter? While I was with my wife?" Tod spat the words at her, true color now suffusing his gaunt face. "Or are you suggesting that we did it together?"

"That's clearly not what I'm saying…" Winnie trailed off, realizing too late that Tod had a reasonable point. Whatever lingering doubts she had about him or about his relationship with Verna, she knew her sister, knew she would never harm her own child. And if Tod had been with Verna all evening, then who…?

"I shouldn't have said that. It was just a gut reaction. After everything that happened when Verna disappeared, I just…" She had no good way to finish the sentence and felt it wouldn't help the situation to say *assumed you really are the awful person I've suspected you might be all along.*

She looked into her sister's wide, frightened eyes, and she felt a jolt of shame at the hurt she saw there. She'd been out of line, and she knew it.

They stood in silence, and the swirling energy that had filled the room moments earlier chilled. Winnie dropped her gaze to a spot on the floor, unwilling to face her sister's accusing eyes. She swallowed once and made a decision that was only partially selfish.

"None of this matters now." She looked at the faces of the bereft parents standing before her. Silent tears ran down Verna's lovely face, and Winnie swallowed a hard lump as she thought of Renata's fine, blond curls and golden eyes, perfect little copies of her mother's. There was no reason to cry, she told herself. Not yet. Not when they knew so little about the situation.

"Let's focus on what we know," she said, heading into the kitchen to pick up the notebook that hung from a magnetic hook on the refrigerator. She noted the time and wrote it at the bottom of the page, adding the comment *Winnie wakes.*

"Now," she said, pushing her white-blond bangs out of her eyes and jutting her chin toward Verna and Tod. "Tell me exactly what happened from the time you walked into the apartment."

Half an hour later, the evening's timeline was fixed in detail, but the three adults whose presence seemed dwarfed by the colossal absence of the family's smallest member were no closer to understanding what might have happened to Ren.

"So, we're all in agreement, then?" Tod asked, looking from one Harvester sister to the other. "Winnie saw her for the last time around ten when she got her a drink and rocked her back to sleep, and then Verna and I walked through the door a little after midnight to find her gone. If someone got into her room after Winnie closed her door, Ren could have disappeared as early as ten-thirty. That's a ninety-minute window for someone to take her. Shorter if that person came through the front door since they would have walked right by Winnie and would have needed to wait until she was sleeping."

The implication of this statement wasn't lost on either of the sisters: taking for granted that whoever took Ren would have needed to use the apartment's main door wasn't reasonable, not in their family's world on which mortal constraints had little bearing.

"What are we going to do, Winnie?" wailed Verna, wilting over the kitchen island and burying her face in her crossed arms. Winnie dropped the notebook she'd been holding on the counter and sidled around the island to her sister's side, draping herself over Verna's back and nuzzling her face against her neck.

"We're going to figure this out, Verna." She spoke the words so quietly that Winnie was sure Tod couldn't make out what she was saying, and the ember of cruelty that rarely flared inside her burned warmly for an instant before fizzling out to shame. "Whatever it takes,

I'm going to figure out what happened to Ren, and I'm going to make sure she comes home to us."

"Oh, Winnie!" Verna choked on a sob and raised herself off the island to wrap her arms around Winnie's waist. Winnie stroked Verna's long, golden hair, murmuring encouragements as her sister's tears created a wet circle on her shoulder. Turning her head, Winnie looked at her brother-in-law, who stood behind his wife. He made eye contact, but his face was pinched closed. Winnie studied him, unsmiling, alternately wishing he'd reach out to comfort his wife and hoping he'd stay on the other side of the kitchen while the sisters comforted one another.

To her surprise, he did the former, moving quietly around the island to press a comforting hand to his wife's shoulder. He didn't try to push Winnie away or pry his wife off her sister, and Winnie, still watching him, smiled weakly in thanks. He dipped his head fractionally in acknowledgement.

A chime interrupted their rare moment of camaraderie. Winnie pulled back from her sister and looked toward the door.

"I'll get it," Tod said, sweeping past his still sniffling wife as he left the kitchen.

Winnie looked questioningly at Verna, who mumbled through lips swollen from crying, "That'll be Mom."

Oh, good. The voice of reason.

Winnie swallowed a put-upon sigh and retrieved a glass from the cabinet to pour Verna an ice water. It would be the first thing their mother would insist on doing—water makes everything better, after all—and she didn't want to be found lacking under Brooke Harvester's critical gaze.

Filling the glass, Winnie heard footsteps behind her as Tod returned to the kitchen. She turned, ready to hold out the water to Verna and intercept their mother and her sometimes-overwhelming ministrations. But to her surprise, the woman who followed Tod into the room wasn't Brooke Harvester, immortal Elemental and master of all waters.

Instead, a stranger stood beside Tod. Winnie gaped. Standing side-by-side, Tod and the gorgeous woman by his side were a study in contrast. While the stranger was Tod's height, in every other regard, she was his precise opposite. This woman was everything pale, black-eyed, lanky Tod wasn't. Her black skin shone with burnished vitality, and her blue eyes, closer in color to Winnie's than any of her sisters' eyes were, studied the two women with cool, critical aloofness. Tod perpetually looked as though he was just coming down with the flu or just getting over it: shadows dusted his cheeks below his eyes, and blue veins webbed his temples. This woman seemed almost too healthy by comparison: her lovely face shone with vibrancy. Winnie fought an intense urge to scan her body from top to bottom. It wasn't that she wanted to ogle this stranger's powerful, robust body—at least it wasn't *just* that—or compare it to her own; rather, she felt the desire to absorb the powerful energy that seemed to flow from the woman.

"Hi," Winnie said lamely, raising the hand not holding Verna's water to waggle her fingers at the newcomer.

The woman tilted her head just slightly, taking in Winnie with an evaluative look that made Winnie rake her fingers through her hair ineffectively.

"You must be Winter," the stranger responded.

This snapped Winnie out of her thrall. She glanced at Verna, who was staring at the newcomer with the same dazed expression Winnie was sure she herself had just been wearing. Verna's face was drawn and bloodless, and her mouth hung open slightly.

"Yes, I'm Winter," she answered tartly. "And you are...?"

"I'm here to help you get your niece back." The woman's voice was smooth and deep, and Winnie felt herself fighting its anesthetizing effect as she challenged the stranger.

"I'm sorry, but who are you exactly? What do you know about my niece?" Suspicion made her eyes narrow. "And who asked you to come here?"

"I did," Tod cut in.

Winnie tore her eyes from the woman, looking at Tod who, truth be told, she'd momentarily forgotten was still standing there. "This is Vita." Tod scratched absently at a non-existent mark on the counter as he mumbled, "She's my sister."

Eleven

"She's your *what*?"

Winnie's head whipped around to take in Verna, who had been staring at her husband and their unknown visitor in pale silence but whose cheeks were now beginning to color from the neck of her blouse up.

"Uh-oh," Winnie cursed under her breath. She dumped the water she had just poured for Verna down the sink. She had seen that creeping flush before, and she knew it was better for everyone in the room if Verna wasn't holding a potential weapon.

Tod continued to pick at the counter, scraping his nail furiously over the same spot as if preparing the kitchen for a visiting health inspector.

"Yeah," he mumbled, refusing to meet his wife's gaze. "Well, it just occurred to me that maybe it made sense to involve my sister. I mean, Ren is her niece too, right?"

Winnie thought she had never heard a silence so threatening as the one Verna wielded against her husband in that moment. She looked from Verna to Tod and back again, plotting with silent arithmetic whether it would be better to hold back Verna, throw her body in front of Tod, or pop a bag of popcorn and enjoy the fisticuffs. She shook herself slightly, fighting what she now suspected was the tranquillizing effect of Tod's sister's power, whatever it may be. She couldn't get distracted by this new Fundamental in the room when Renata's safety was at stake.

"Okay," she said calmly, raising her hands in placation and stepping between the seething form of her sister and the slowly receding body of Tod. "Okay, let's just take this one step at a time—"

"To hell with that!" Verna roared, pressing viciously against the island and slapping its surface with both hands. "To hell with one step at a time, Winnie! I want to know who this chick is and what she's doing in my kitchen!"

"'Chick'?" Vita echoed, her mouth contorted in a sneer. "I don't know who you think—"

"No one is talking to you!" Verna cut through Vita's complaint with a growl that made Winnie draw back in alarm.

Apparently, Tod felt similarly. "Maybe we should all—"

"Maybe you—!" Verna pointed an accusatory finger at Tod. "And you—!" She now swung the finger of condemnation in Vita's direction. "Should get the hell out of my kitchen before I do something you'll regret!" Verna shrieked, and Winnie, sensing that Verna was entering a phase of distress that could only be labeled *pre-apocalyptic*, reached toward Tod and Vita, hoping that between the two of them they had enough sense to back out of the kitchen without saying another word.

They did not.

In a burst of near-deafening cacophony, the distraught couple and the newly-revealed sibling let loose with impassioned tirades. Verna's already flushed face burned crimson, her swollen eyes flashing hotly as she screeched. Vita, her deep voice sounding a counterpoint to Verna's increasingly high pitch, pushed her brother aside to press against the opposite side of the island, gesticulating as she attempted to talk both faster and louder than her sister-in-law. Tod, having forgotten about the offending spot on the countertop, managed to demonstrate the depth of his inability to read a room by alternating between cheering on his wife and his sister, despite the fact they were arguing against one another.

"—think I'm going to stand being called a—"

"—you've haven't been here for anything else in her life, so what makes you think—"

"—should be thankful I even agreed to come here in the first—"

"—must not be that close considering he's never even mentioned—"

Winnie tried to track the exchange from one woman to the other, glancing occasionally at Tod when he managed to make his voice heard over the women's dominating shouts. She was desperate to leap to her sister's aid, but Verna didn't need her help at the moment, and even as her mind raced to come up with arguments to support Verna, a persistent thought at the back of her mind urged with greater and greater urgency that this was all a waste time that would be better spent using any resource available to search for Ren.

Perhaps Vita was exactly the resource they needed. Perhaps that's why Tod—loath though Winnie was to give him credit for having a helpful plan—had called her in the first place.

But maybe she isn't, a smaller voice inside Winnie's head murmured. *Maybe there's a reason she showed up tonight. Maybe she got here so quickly because this isn't the first time she's been here tonight...*

Winnie shook her head, desperate to clear it so that she could focus on what needed to be done right now. Grabbing her sister's flailing arm, she tried to interject, managing only to add one more layer of unhelpful noise to the now incomprehensible din in the small kitchen.

They might have gone on like that half the night if a sudden, piercing whistle hadn't cut through the din like an emergency klaxon, startling the four of them into silence and prompting Winnie to clap her hands protectively over her ears. Tearing her attention from the knot of people surrounding the little island, she looked up into eyes the color of tidepools.

Brooke Harvester stood in the doorway, looking from one face to the next, her small, perfectly-manicured hands on her narrow hips, her made-up face looking dew-kissed and morning-fresh despite the microwave clock reading a little after two a.m.

"Uh-oh," Winnie said for the second time that hour, and behind the island, concealed from their mother's keen stare, the two sisters clasped each other's hand.

"What exactly is going on here?" Brooke asked.

Winnie noticed that Vita, as startled as the rest of them had been at Brooke's two-fingered whistle, had regained her composure and now gazed coolly at the petite force of nature before her. If Brooke was intimidated by having to look up in order to return the considerably-taller woman's stare, she didn't show it.

"Well?" Brooke prompted them again, and Winnie noted with scorn that Tod had found the forgotten spot on the island to resume picking at. She resisted a strong urge to reach across the counter and slap his hand.

"Mom, someone took Ren," Verna whispered, and Winnie marveled at her powerful, reserved mother, whose eyes widened only slightly at this news.

Brooke breathed deeply several times, studying her daughter before turning her gaze on Winnie. "You were babysitting tonight, I believe? And this happened on your watch?"

Winnie felt her face burn, but she held her mother's gaze defiantly. "Yes. It happened after I'd tucked her in. She and I were both asleep." She felt Verna squeeze her hand, and Winnie squeezed back, thankful to have her sister there beside her as she faced down their mother's wrath.

"I see," Brooke responded finally. Her head swiveled to face Vita. "And what exactly do you know about this?" she asked with the tone of a teacher grilling witnesses to a schoolyard mishap.

"What makes you think I know anything?" Vita answered. "And even if I did know something, what makes you think I'd tell you?" Winnie gulped audibly. Vita was either brave or foolish. Possibly both. They could debate it at her funeral.

Brooke hadn't changed position since the charged silence following the screaming match had settled over the room, but at these words, one of her beautifully shaped eyebrows rose slowly until it disappeared under her side-swept bangs.

Winnie felt a shiver run from the small of her back up her spine.

"I think you know something because you're a stranger in my daughter's home on the night her daughter disappeared. That seems like a suspicious coincidence to me, and I don't even believe in coincidences. And I know you're going to tell me what you know because if you think whatever cutesy little power you have rolling off of you right now is impressive, then you haven't played with the grown-ups yet." Brooke looked the statuesque newcomer up and down, unimpressed. "Honey, I'm the grown-up that makes other grown-ups pack up their toys and go home."

Winnie squeezed Verna's hand again, not for reassurance this time but to stop herself from clapping.

To Vita's credit, she didn't look away from her diminutive opponent, but there was no mistaking the palpable shift in the kitchen's atmosphere. Vita's powers, so mesmerizing and pervasive when she'd entered the kitchen, seemed to roll back like a carpet, and Winnie felt the concern and anxiety that had been dampened since Vita's arrival begin to swamp her again.

Verna surely felt the same effect, Winnie thought, when a moment later her sister sagged against her, her face again drained of color and silent tears running down over her pale cheeks.

"Come on," Winnie said to the room in general. "Let's go sit down. Then Vita can tell us why she's here and what she knows about Ren."

Several minutes later, four of them were gathered in uneasy silence in the living room, the smell of brewing coffee wafting in from the kitchen where Brooke puttered efficiently, preparing a coffee tray. She'd scolded Winnie—predictably—when she'd discovered Verna had had nothing to eat or drink since the discovery of Ren's empty bed, and after supervising her third-born's consumption of a full glass of water, she'd shooed them all into the living room to settle Verna into a club chair with her feet up on an ottoman and a blanket tucked around her slender shoulders.

Vita sat regally in the wing chair across the seating from Verna, her long legs crossed at the knee and her hands hanging languidly off either armrest. That left the small sofa for Winnie and Tod, who perched at either end, as far from one another as possible, Winnie with her legs crossed toward her sister so that she could administer help as needed, and Tod on the edge of the cushion, leaning forward with his forearms on his knees, clearly ready to leap up at the first hint of Verna's distress. Verna was oblivious to both attendants.

"Everyone have some coffee and half a sandwich," Brooke instructed, her tone making it clear that each of them was expected to comply. Drowsiness and low blood sugar were not going to impede the search for Brooke's granddaughter.

Like grudgingly obedient children, they each took a cup and a triangular sandwich from the tray. Winnie would have said the last thing she wanted was to eat, but when she bit into the cucumber and mayonnaise sandwich, she realized that she was, in fact, peckish, and the hot coffee warmed a spot in her chest she hadn't realized was chilled.

"Now," Brooke began with the tone of a chairperson calling a meeting to order. She had settled down in the space between Winnie and Tod. "I reviewed Winnie's notes in the kitchen while the coffee brewed." Verna caught Winnie's eye, and they shared a sisterly look that said *Mom...am I right?* "I'm caught up on what happened tonight. I'm here because Verna texted me to say there was an emergency, and I should come over right away. I'd like to know why you're here." She inclined her head toward Vita, who raised her chin in a motion that could be interpreted forgivingly as acknowledgement and unforgivingly as defiance. Winnie hoped her mother was in the forgiving mood, but she wouldn't have put money on it.

"I'm here because my brother called me and asked me to come," Vita responded, and Winnie noticed a tiny spasm of surprise cross her mother's face before it settled once again into stern serenity.

"Is that so? Tod failed to mention he had a sister. Failed to mention it in the four years that he's been married to my daughter, I mean." She turned her attention to Tod, though she didn't address him directly. "Perhaps he was planning to mention you when Ren graduated from college."

Neither Tod nor Vita acknowledged this, either to explain or defend it. Vita continued to stare fixedly at Brooke, and Tod watched his wife with dour intensity.

"Why would Tod call you? I only ask because it seems unusual to me that, in a crisis, he would call someone he's never mentioned even to his own wife, someone who's never visited or apparently wanted any contact with the child he's calling to report missing."

Winnie cringed at her mother's barbed words, but if they stung Vita, she didn't let on.

"My brother and I aren't close. Never have been. But he called me because he knows that I make it my business to keep an eye on the person who'd be most likely to cause problems in our lives."

Winnie's eyes narrowed as she studied Vita's dark, striking features. What kind of dissembling was this? She opened her eyes to ask, but Verna beat her to it.

"What's that supposed to mean? Who'd want to cause us problems? Who would do something like this?"

Besides you, quite possibly, Winnie wanted to add, but she wisely refrained. It wouldn't help the situation to get snarky now.

"Our father, Damion Strife."

Winnie noted the swift narrowing of her mother's eyes, but she was so taken aback by Vita's accusation that she simply tucked the realization that Brooke recognized the name into the back of her mind for later examination. Foremost in her thoughts was the idea that Tod had a lot of explaining to do when this was all over.

And then a thought pushed all the others aside: the name Strife.

"But your last name isn't Strife," she said to Tod. She could feel her mother's burning gaze, a silent reprimand for focusing on patronymics of all things.

"No," Tod answered without looking at her. His attention was focused on his hands clasped between his knees. Winnie couldn't blame him: every woman in this room was unimpressed with him right now. "Vita and I use our mother's name."

Winnie didn't judge that decision. She certainly liked Renata Kreis more than Renata Strife.

"I see," said Brooke, shooting a pointed look at Winnie. "And what makes you think Strife is responsible for my granddaughter's disappearance?"

"Well, there's the fact that he's a bastard who enjoys destruction, decay, and discord," Vita responded.

Brooke cleared her throat in tacit disapproval of Vita's choice of words, but Vita didn't seem to notice, or perhaps she simply didn't care about Brooke's sensitivity to impropriety. Winnie guessed the latter; she doubted much escaped Vita's lively, intense gaze.

"But, there's also the fact that two nights ago he left his apartment in Tokyo and hasn't been seen since."

Tod's head shot up at this. "What?"

"That's right, little brother. So, I'm going to suggest he should be the first person you track down."

"Wait a minute," Winnie interrupted, trying to look objectively at the evidence despite her desire to clutch at any lead that presented itself, no matter how meager. "Just because your dad left his apartment, is that really a reason to suspect he might be involved in a kidnapping?"

"Considering he hasn't left it in nine years, I'd say it's a damn good reason," Vita snapped back. Winnie felt equal parts irritated by her tone and impressed by her fearless assertiveness.

"I agree," Brooke interjected. "Where did he go?"

"I lost him. I was preparing to head to Japan to track him down when I got the call from Tod."

Winnie's shoulders slumped at this news, and Vita directed her next words at Winnie.

"We'll be able to find him, and I'm confident that when we do, we'll find..." She waved her hand vaguely.

"Renata!" Winnie scowled. "Your niece's name is Renata."

"Renata," Vita repeated, not looking the least embarrassed at having forgotten Ren's name. "We need to look for chaos, decay, filth...Those things follow him everywhere he goes. Those things and...others."

Winnie felt a prickle of trepidation. What wasn't Vita telling them?

Perhaps nothing but what's in the script, she thought. *Just like Mom said, it's too coincidental. She shows up tonight of all nights with a ready-made lead for us to follow...*

It's a trap.

Winnie's face flushed at the thought. If Vita really were working with her father, and he stole Ren, was the idea simply to use something of value to lure the real target out? And who was that target likely to be?

Before Winnie could parse her complicated thoughts, Verna sat forward, the blanket falling from her shoulders. "You're joking, right? That's your advice? 'Go where there's chaos'? Do you not understand that my daughter is with this awful person you're describing?" Verna's voice crept slowly up into the shrill register it had climbed into during their screaming match, and both Winnie and Brooke leaned forward simultaneously to comfort her, Winnie stroking her back as Brooke picked up her glass of water from the coffee table and eased it into Verna's hand.

Returning her gaze to Vita, Brooke began, "I think it might be helpful to think about other ways of—"

Verna cut off her mother's sentence with a shriek, dropping her water glass on the hardwood and drawing her legs up into the chair like a cartoon housewife fleeing a scurrying mouse. Winnie shot up, rushing to Verna's side.

"Verna!" she cried. "What's wrong?"

Verna clutched her sister. "Winnie!" she shrieked. "My water! There was a face in it!"

Twelve

Winnie tore her eyes from Verna's shocked expression and looked at the puddle of water at her feet.

"A face? Verna, was it Nina?"

Verna gaped at her sister. "Of course it wasn't Nina, Winnie! Don't you think I would have recognized her? Anyway, what would she be doing in my water glass? How would she have gotten there?"

Across the room, Vita cleared her throat. "Someone going to catch me up, here?"

"Nina Ramirez, a friend of Winnie's," Tod supplied, motioning with a tip of his head in the general direction of the Depths. "She's the caretaker who took my place down there so that I could live here with my family."

"That's big of her," Vita answered, squinting suspiciously. "What's she getting out of it?"

"Nina isn't like that," Winnie shot back, bristling at the suggestion that her friend could have ulterior motives. "Nina's got a heart of gold. She likes being helpful, and she likes trying new things."

"Is that from her online dating profile?" Vita countered with a smirk, and Winnie glared at her furiously. Turning back to Verna, Winnie endeavored to ignore Vita…for now.

"What did the face look like, Verna? Are you sure it wasn't anyone you recognized?"

"I'm sure." She had calmed down since her scare, climbing out of the chair over its arm to avoid the puddle of water on the floor.

"Tod, who else down there has the ability to use your pool? I thought the only people you authorized were Nina and Ab—Mom, don't!" The motion of Brooke dropping to one knee caught her attention. "Don't wipe up the water!"

Brooke peered up at Winnie in surprise. "Why on earth not, Winter? It'll ruin the hardwood."

"Or someone could slip and get hurt," Vita added pointedly, and Winnie noted the blush that suffused her mother's pale cheeks at the subtle jab.

"Yes, or someone could slip and get hurt," she repeated with dignity, leaning forward once again to mop up the puddle.

Winnie grabbed her wrist just in time. "Mom, whoever that was in the water is obviously trying to make contact with us."

"Or watching us," Vita added, and four heads turned in unison to stare at her.

"What?" she asked, looking from one surprised face to the next in serene appraisal. Winnie couldn't help thinking she seemed to be enjoying the audience she'd gathered.

"What's that supposed to mean?" Winnie challenged, Vita's impugnment of Nina's character still fresh in her mind.

But before Vita could answer, Brooke cut across her. "Whatever she means, it's all the more reason this needs to go," and before Winnie could stop her, Brooke flung out the towel over the small puddle and wiped away the offending mess.

"Ugh, Mom!" Winnie lamented, raking her fingers through her choppy hair in frustration. It was so dirty from the long night and having been slept on that the motion sent it spiking up in every direction. She puffed up her cheeks and blew out an exasperated raspberry.

"Winnie, don't be crass," Brooke scolded as she carried the drenched towel into the kitchen and wrung it out into the sink.

Winnie glared at her back as she retreated and then marched into the kitchen after her. There was no point in pursuing the argument; Winnie was certain her mother's insistence on defying her had more to do with her irritation at being shown up by Vita than with Winnie's request. She brushed past her mother and opened the cabinet, pulling out a shallow pasta bowl and standing beside Brooke, waiting patiently for her mother to stand aside.

Brooke was wiping out the sink with the towel she'd used to mop up the puddle, and when she finished, she carefully rinsed the sink, turned off the water, and wrung out the towel once again. Then, she folded it once and hung it over the faucet. Looking around with her wet hands still dripping into the sink, she noted the bowl in Winnie's hand. Then she bent to look around her at the stovetop. "Winter, hand me the pot on the stove, and I'll finish washing up."

Winnie swallowed her first response and did her best to smile at her mother, though from the sour look on Brooke's face, she suspected it wasn't a very convincing smile. "Before you do that, can I just fill this up? Please?" she added, patting herself on the head mentally for handling herself so maturely.

Brooke returned what Winnie suspected was her own tight smile and stepped fractionally to one side, holding her hands dramatically over the sink to make sure Winnie could observe how inconvenient this request was proving.

Winnie looked back over her shoulder to make sure the others were still in the living room; then she turned to her mother. Brooke might be in a mood, but Winnie needed answers to some questions.

"Mom," she hissed in a whisper. "You recognized that name, Strife. Who is he? Do you know him?"

Her mother stiffened, and Winnie feared she might refuse to answer. Like the waters she commanded, Brooke Harvester could be capricious.

But to her relief, her mother cast her own quick glance over her shoulder before leaning in to answer Winnie, resting her wet hands on the lip of the sink to close the space between them.

"Yes, I know him. Or...I did. It's been many generations since I saw him last. He's the main reason your father and I made the decision to keep you girls away from Others like us." She looked pointedly at her daughter. "Not all of the Others *are* like us. And Strife is the best example of that."

"What do you mean?"

"Each Other serves a purpose, Winter. Our line is productive. We change matter from one form to another: season to season, water to ice..." Winnie nodded to signal she understood what her mother meant. "Some Others are more…destructive."

"And that includes Strife?"

"Yes. Death has to exist, Winter. Things must rot and decay. Fear, anger, envy…those are forces that balance out the universe. And Fundamentals have to maintain that balance."

Winnie considered her mother's words carefully. She'd never thought of the lives of mortals in these terms, but perhaps it was time she started.

"If Strife really is behind this, what do you think he's trying to achieve? Why would he take Ren?"

"I don't know," Brooke admitted, her lovely face pale under her makeup. "The last time I saw him, he was…"

Winnie studied her face anxiously. "He was what, Mom?"

Brooke sighed. "He was angry with me for rejecting him."

Winnie's eyes widened. "Mom! Are you saying you and he were…that the two of you…?"

Brooke looked blandly at her daughter. "Get your mind out of the gutter, Winter. He and your father were both pursuing me, and when I made my choice, Damion was angry. Frankly, that anger was part of the reason I rejected him. That and…," she trailed off, her eyes losing focus as she looked at something, or someone, Winnie couldn't see.

"And…?" Winnie prompted.

"I'd seen the Other he replaced. He'd been destroyed, and Damion had coalesced to take his place.

He was young and fresh then, but the Other he replaced was revolting, and I wondered if, over time..." She snapped back into the present and sighed at Winnie's perplexed expression. "Maybe your father and I should have shared more of the Others with you girls. But there's no time now. Just know that if Damion's position has done to him what it did to the one who came before him—"

"Winnie?" Verna called weakly from the other room.

Brooke turned away from her daughter, and Winnie knew that whatever information she'd gotten was likely to be all she'd get tonight. She turned on the faucet.

The bowl filled, she headed back toward the living room.

"Winter, dear?" Brooke said from behind her, where she'd resumed tidying.

"Yes, Mother?"

"Try not to let that end up all over the floor again."

Winnie exercised a level of self-control that should have earned her a trophy.

"I'll do my very best," she replied, and turned to leave the kitchen. Had she noticed Vita's gaze upon her, she might not have rolled her eyes quite so dramatically, but it wasn't until after that almost-painful eye-roll that she felt the weighty stare of the stranger in their midst. Winnie's gut twisted at the unnerving serenity in those umber eyes, but she resisted the urge to look away. This was *her* family after all, at least in the sense that she was the one who'd been there when

Vita hadn't, and she wasn't about to let some newcomer cow her.

But as he held Vita's gaze, she realized Vita wasn't trying to intimidate her; on the contrary, something in the other woman's expression seemed almost sympathetic. Her expression seemed to say *I'm right there with you, sister.*

The kind of expression she would have if she'd been spending a lot of time lately with an angry father, Winnie told herself. If that were the case, knowing what she did now about her parents' history with Strife, had she answered her own question about who might be the real target of Strife's plot?

"Winnie," Verna spoke, breaking into Winnie's thoughts and pulling her attention away from Vita's stare. "What are you doing?"

Winnie set the bowl of water on the table. When she sneaked another look at Vita, the newcomer was studying the framed pictures on the end table beside the couch, apparently uninterested in the other people in the room.

"I'm calling Nina," Winnie responded. "If someone in the Depths is using Tod's anchor pool, Nina should know about it, right?"

"That's a good idea," Verna answered her, and Winnie felt a knot tighten in her gut. If this didn't work, not only would they still not have any leads on Ren, but she'd have lifted Verna's hopes only to dash them. As worried as Winnie felt, she could only imagine how amplified the fear and anxiety must be for her sister.

Pausing in her movements, she reached across the small space of the sitting area and clutched Verna's hand. "Verna, I don't know if Nina can help, but it seems pretty suspicious to me that on the same night Ren disappeared, someone tried making contact through Tod's pool. If this doesn't work, we'll figure something else out. And we'll just keep figuring things out until we have Renata back. That's exactly what I did to find you. Okay?"

Verna choked on a sob and nodded in assent, squeezing Winnie's hand like a lifeline.

Winnie turned back to the bowl she'd set on the table, perching on the edge of the armchair so that she could look down into it. "I need everyone to give me a finger," she said, gazing about at her audience.

Vita snorted, and both Winnie and Verna shot her a dirty look.

"Are you here to help us or not?" Winnie asked coolly.

Vita huffed cattily. "Fine. Do I get to pick which finger I give you?"

Winnie held up her index finger rather than risking opening her mouth. She dipped the tip in the shallow bowl and held it there as Tod, Verna, and finally Vita did the same. Drawing her magic around herself, she whispered "Show us Nina."

The four of them gazed into the bowl in silence. As if in mockery, the bowl showed them nothing at all.

Thirteen

"Are you sure you know how to do this?" Vita asked, her tone unimpressed.

Winnie withdrew her finger from the water and turned to Tod. "What's going on, Tod? Where's Nina? Why isn't this showing us anything?"

Tod, having withdrawn his finger as well, sat quietly studying the still surface of the makeshift anchor pool.

"I don't know," he answered quietly.

"You *don't know*?" Winnie tried to tamp down the note of panic in her voice, but the stress of the night and her lack of sleep had worn her nerves down to raw nubs. "How can you not *know*?"

"I *don't know* why I don't know, Winnie. I just don't," Tod responded tetchily.

"Well, what does it normally mean when nothing shows up in an anchor pool?"

Tod looked at her blankly. "Something always shows up."

Winnie felt her poorly-controlled anger surge. "That doesn't seem to be entirely true now, does it?" she snapped, raking her fingers through her hair.

"What is going on in here?" Brooke asked, striding out of the kitchen at the sound of Winnie's raised voice.

It had also roused Tod, who stood and stared down at Winnie imperiously.

"What do you want me to say, Winnie? This has never happened before. I don't know any more than you do."

Winnie stood too, though her own imperiousness was somewhat diminished by the sizable height differential between them; she had to look up his nose in order to look down her own at him.

"Well, you need to figure it out!" she insisted. "This is your medium. You're the expert. Expert your way to a solution."

"Winter!" Brooke scolded. "I don't think there's any reason to raise our voices. Surely we can talk about this calmly…"

Winnie turned to her mother, anger swirling like a fog around her, but though she opened her mouth to respond, it was Verna who spoke next.

"Oh, stop clutching your pearls, Mother! Who cares about raised voices? My baby is missing, and we can't reach Nina, and someone who shouldn't be in Nina's pool is clearly watching us! Don't you think we have the right to be a little hysterical?"

Winnie gawped at her sister, wide-eyed. Brooke regarded Verna as well, though her expression conveyed somewhat less bald admiration and somewhat more calculated appraisal.

After several silent beats, Brooke turned that terrifying stare on Tod, who drew back fractionally.

"Tod," she said calmly, her mastery of imperiousness exposing what he and Winnie had been playing at moments before as paltry imitation. "Put your wife to bed. Then follow her there. I'm calling Pete, and he and I are going to find Nina and straighten out this mess."

A confusing gabble of voices erupted at this. Verna's cry of refusal matched Tod's, who seemed to find it insulting that his mother-in-law had essentially tried to put him down for a nap. Winnie's wild protestation became lost in the cacophony, but she did her best to object, though she could hardly explain her fear that Pete and Brooke might very well be the two people Strife and Vita sought to maneuver into place. Instead, she repeated the same wisdom Brooke herself had imparted when they'd discovered Verna was being held in the Depths: it was one thing for the girls, beings of lesser power, to trespass into that other realm, but it was something else entirely for the monumental powers that were her mom and dad to go there. And that *something else* was enough to frighten even her rock of a father.

Somehow, Brooke picked her argument out of the din and turned to her.

"I'll remind you, Winter, that it was I who assisted you the last time. Surely you haven't forgotten that?" Brooke's eyes blazed dangerously.

"I haven't forgotten, Mom." Winnie lowered her voice. "But you knew I was there. You and Dad were both tapped into your elements, searching for the opportunity to help me. You said yourself that if I hadn't used anchor pool water to do what I did, you likely wouldn't have even known I'd needed help or where to send it. And the help you did provide exhausted you, Mother! That was just a nudge of magic from a long distance. You're talking about walking through the door and announcing your presence!"

"If your father and I go together—"

"Then we risk losing both of you!" Winnie had to make Brooke see sense. If this really was a trap, she had to keep them away from Strife.

"If you think—"

"Shut up, both of you." Vita's voice cut through the room like a scythe. All three Harvester women turned to stare at her. "Tod and I are going. The rest of you can stay here."

"No," Winnie and Brooke said in unison, and Brooke caught Winnie's eye to confirm their united objection: no rescue party would leave the apartment without at least one Harvester in its ranks.

"I'll come too," Winnie volunteered before Brooke could. Though her lips pressed into a tense line, the Harvester family matriarch didn't object.

Vita seemed to consider this, and Winnie wondered if she was actually working out the next several moves in whatever game she was playing. She'd agreed a little too readily to Brooke staying behind.

Because Pete's the real prize?

She pushed away the thought. She couldn't focus on figuring out Vita's schemes as long as Ren was out there somewhere, frightened and alone.

"Fine," Vita said at last, looking Winnie up and down appraisingly. "Is that what you're going to wear?"

As day broke, Winnie, Tod, and Vita stepped out onto the street. Brooke had insisted Verna lie down, and though Verna had been sure she wouldn't be able to sleep, Winnie had heard her snoring when she checked on her before leaving. It had taken only a few minutes to decide on a plan once the rescue party was agreed upon: Brooke would stay at the apartment to tend to Verna while Tod, Vita, and Winnie went to the nearest portal to the Depths and slipped over to that other place to investigate. Before leaving, Winnie reminded her mother that time moved differently there, so she shouldn't worry if they didn't get word back immediately.

"I have to stop at my apartment," Winnie told Vita and Tod as they turned to head up the street. Tod shot her an irritated look. "I need to change clothes and get some stuff in case we're gone a while."

"There's a pool near your building," Tod finally conceded. "We'll stop on the way. Too bad you couldn't have borrowed some clothes from your sister. It would have saved us some time."

Winnie returned his irritated look at this, and in the process caught Vita's eye as she walked on the other side of her brother. Vita was studying Tod with a look similar to Winnie's, and Winnie felt a grudging camaraderie with this woman who definitely knew Tod was taking a jab at Winnie—she could never fit into her taller and slenderer sister's clothing—and who also clearly didn't approve of this criticism. But she did her best to quash it: wouldn't it serve Vita's purpose to win Winnie's trust?

"I get you've had a bad night, brother," Vita said, "but try to resist the urge to be an insufferable douchebag."

Tod scowled. Winnie snorted. She shouldn't like Vita, but she was finding it hard to dislike her. Being near Vita made Winnie feel…energized? Hopeful? She couldn't quite articulate the feeling, but it was somehow good. Somehow…healthy.

Winnie stopped dead, whacking her forehead.

"You're health!" she exclaimed. "Jeez. Duh," she rolled her eyes. "Carry on. I'm caught up now." She started walking again, and Vita smirked.

"Glad to see you've finally joined us," she said, but her tone was good-natured, and Winnie grinned at her around Tod despite her better judgement.

"Yes. Terrific," Tod intoned snarkily. "You guys can go get your nails done when this is over."

He was saved from an equally snarky reply from one or both women by Winnie's phone ringing. She snatched it from her purse, anticipating Brooke or Verna on the other end, but surprisingly, Nolan's name appeared on the screen.

"Uh-oh," Winnie muttered. The thrill she normally felt when Nolan called was replaced by a sinking dread. In all the excitement of Ren's disappearance and Vita's arrival, she'd overlooked Nolan entirely, and it was very likely that he wasn't calling her this early on a Saturday morning for idle chitchat but rather because he'd already discovered his sister wasn't where she was supposed to be.

Nolan was nice and single and quite funny, really (now that he no longer feared she was dangerously unhinged), but Winnie remembered all too well how angry he'd been the first time they'd met. Then, she'd at least had answers to his questions; this time, she'd have to admit Nina might be in real trouble, the kind he'd been concerned about her getting into from the moment he'd learned about her job in the Depths.

What finally made her tap the green answer icon was the shameful admission that she owed Nolan the truth, and this time he deserved it from the beginning rather than an apologetic summary after the fact.

"Nolan," she said, putting the phone to her ear and slowing a bit. Tod and Vita strode ahead, their heads oriented toward one another in muted conversation. Winnie's brow furrowed as she watched them, but Nolan's voice cut off her curiosity about their conversation.

"Hey, Winnie. Sorry to call so early—"

"I'm up. I've been up," she broke in, and almost added *for hours and hours* before biting her tongue. As Vita and Tod pulled farther ahead, Winnie felt those hours more heavily, and it seemed her feet began moving slower. She studied Vita's back, watching her springy, natural curls bounce as she moved and admiring the strong jaw and glowing skin revealed by her fade. Feeling like something she should have figured out a while ago was clicking into place, she jogged to catch up and was unsurprised to discover that, when she got within a few feet of Vita's regal form, her step quickened, and she felt as if the weariness of the long night was draining away.

"…which is why I thought I'd check with you." She realized Nolan was still speaking and forced her attention back to his call.

"Say that again, Nolan? I missed some of it." Winnie grimaced as Nolan sighed peevishly.

"Which part?"

"Umm..."

"I said I'm trying to find out why I haven't heard from Nina. Have you heard from her? I know it's early, but she and I check in at the same time every day, and I haven't heard from her today."

"I see," Winnie stalled, wracking her brains to figure out what to say and what to hold back. She didn't want to frighten Nolan, but if roles were reversed, she'd certainly want to know anything he knew about her best friend's whereabouts. "I...uh...Well, about Nina..."

"What about Nina?" Nolan's tone became sharp, and Winnie girded herself for the inevitable.

"Nolan, something may be wrong. I don't know any more than that right now, but I'm on my way to her right now to see what's going on."

"On your way? You mean...*down there?*"

Winnie rolled her eyes. Nolan tended to sound a bit Puritanical when he spoke of the Depths, but she tried to remind herself that his understanding of existence and after-existence was informed primarily by people with firsthand knowledge of only one of those states.

"Yes, *down there*," she responded. "Look, Nolan, I have to tell you the truth. My niece went missing overnight, and we have reason to suspect someone might have taken her to the Depths. So, we're on our way there—"

"Who's *we*?" Nolan interrupted.

"Well," Winnie hesitated, anticipating Nolan's response. "There's me, obviously, and Vita, whom you don't know, and...Tod."

"Tod??" Nolan said this so loudly that Winnie yanked the phone away from her ear, wincing. Through the line, she heard what seemed to be spluttering and the false starts of several sentences. Tod cast a glance back over his shoulder, perhaps rightly thinking he'd heard his name. Winnie glanced away, feigning interest in a sign for a beer she'd never heard of that was taped in the front window of a convenience store they were passing.

She put the phone back to her ear when Nolan seemed to have regained his ability to make complete and sensible sentences.

"Have you lost your freaking mind?" he demanded. Nolan was articulate now, but not exactly calm.

He was taking this better than she thought he would.

"You're letting that undead sack of trash lead the search for my sister?"

"Ix-nay on the ash-tray," Winnie side-mouthed into the phone.

Ahead of her, she heard Vita mumble a side-mouth comment of her own: "I wouldn't have pegged your sister-in-law as a smoker."

Tod responded with a shrug and a grunt. Apparently, Vita's reviving magic didn't have the energizing effect on him that it did on Winnie.

"I'll nix nothing, Winnie. Nothing!" Nolan was still fired up, and Winnie was preparing to soothe him when the entirety of his comment struck her.

"What makes you think I'm letting anyone else take the lead?" Winnie stopped walking, and at the sound of her raised voice, Tod and Vita paused to look back at her. They doubled back to follow her side of the conversation. "I'm the one who has experience rescuing someone from the Depths, you know."

Nolan went quiet, and Winnie practically heard his eyes narrow through the phone.

"Are you saying I should be reassured that the woman who got my sister into this crap-ton of mayhem has teamed up with the predator who caused the mayhem in the first place to make sure my only sister is okay?"

Winnie was silent for a beat. "Well, when you put it that way, it sounds like a terrible idea."

"That's because it *is* a terrible idea!" Winnie had to jerk the phone away from her face again.

"I suppose you have a better one?" she offered as rejoinder.

"You're damn right I do," Nolan said. "I'm coming with you. Stay right where you are until I get there." The call ended.

Winnie looked at the phone before glancing up at her brother-in-law, whose sharp features looked even sharper in the warm morning light. Vita glanced back and forth between them with mild curiosity.

In her hand, Winnie's phone vibrated, alerting her to a new text. It was from Nolan.

It occurs to me I should have asked this before I hung up but where are you exactly?

Winnie texted back her address, figuring they'd be there by the time Nolan made it across town.

Fine, he responded. *Like I said stay there til I get there.*

Winnie snorted, combing back her hair and puffing up her cheeks. When her phone vibrated again, she groaned.

Also do you think I'll need a jacket?

Fourteen

Winnie marched the unlikely siblings, in whose company she would prefer not to be, up the stairs to her apartment. It was the first time Tod had been to her place since the day not long after her return from the Depths when she'd come home to find him attempting to use her apartment as a temporary flophouse while his wife considered the ramifications of her decision to marry the death Fundamental.

He was, she decided, as welcome now as he had been then. But thinking of that night put her in mind of the time that had elapsed and of the many things that had happened in the years since she'd first returned from the Depths. She had sweet Ren in her life now, for one thing, and she had a stronger bond with her best friend Nina than she ever could have imagined she would, given the fact that Nina was a mortal. And of course, she was getting to know Nolan better...

"I need to take a shower and change my clothes," she said over her shoulder to Tod and Vita, leaving them to their frosty companionship as she took off into her bedroom and closed the door. Brooke would have been appalled at her daughter's lack of hospitality, but Winnie found that she simply didn't care. They were capable adults, after all; they didn't need her to tell them where to sit or how to get a drink if they wanted one.

The moment the door clicked shut after Winnie's departure, Tod whirled to face his sister.

"What the hell are you doing here, Vita?" he whisper-hissed. "What are you up to? It's time for you to explain yourself."

"Me?" Vita whispered back incredulously. "I'm the one who needs to explain myself? Why don't *you* start by explaining how you ended up married to an Elemental? My sources tell me you abducted her—"

"Oh, please," Tod interrupted, sneering. "Your *spies,* you mean? You're more like the old man than you like to admit. None of that has anything to do with this."

"Doesn't it?" Vita's eyes blazed in challenge, and Tod turned away under the heat of his sister's scrutiny.

"Did you know our father was going to do this?" he asked her quietly, moving aside the sheers to stare unseeingly out the window.

Vita snorted. "If he was going to collude with one of us, it wouldn't be me." She crossed her arms stubbornly over her chest.

"Maybe not in the past," Tod responded. "But I don't know what you've been up to the last century or so...How would I know whether the two of you have formed an alliance? How do I know you two haven't been plotting this?"

Vita didn't respond but only sneered at her brother.

With renewed vigor, Tod moved back across the room to confront her. "It seems pretty obvious to me that you've been keeping tabs on me, dear sister. You knew about Verna, and you knew my daughter had been kidnapped. What else do you know? And what exactly have you been telling the old man?"

Vita snorted again, but she didn't back away from her brother. "Let me be real clear about this, Tod. I keep tabs on both of you for my own security and for the safety of the people we have an obligation to protect. Don't stand there and pretend that I don't have a very good reason to do so after the tricks the two of you have pulled…"

Tod's eyes thinned to slits, and his otherwise sallow skin reddened in a flush that crept up from the neck of his tee-shirt.

"That's all in the past. I turned my back on the old man when he hung me out to dry with the Council of the Others. Let's not forget that your hands aren't exactly clean either. Now you want me to believe you're concerned about the welfare of a kid you've never even met before?"

Vita held her brother's gaze, and when she spoke, her words were clipped, their carefully enunciated syllables belying the calm passivity of her features.

"You've brought something unknown into the world, Tod. Something with the potential for misuse, for danger. None of us knows what powers your daughter might have, but one thing I do know is that Others outside our family are already scheming to find ways to use her to their advantage. I'm here to make sure Others *inside* our family aren't planning to do the same thing."

"So you say," he spat back. "But isn't that exactly the story you'd use if you were here on our father's orders?"

Vita gave her brother a withering look before turning away from him and striding to the front door without a backward glance.

"I'll be downstairs waiting," she said. Stepping through the door, she paused and looked back. "Don't make me wait."

Half an hour later, the two siblings and the perturbed sister-in-law stood in a loose, unspeaking group in front of Winnie's building, watching the lean, dark-haired figure of Nolan Ramirez hurrying up the street toward them. Winnie watched his approach, his slender legs carrying him on a determined path through the sparse crowd of dog-walkers and office workers on their way to buildings downtown. In spite of her jangled nerves, she couldn't help admiring the pleasant breadth of his shoulders and the endearing bounce of his curly hair. There was something jerky about his movements; when he bumped into a woman who had stopped unexpectedly on the sidewalk in front of him, he sprang back like an excited puppy as he both apologized and steered her rather brazenly out of his path.

He caught Winnie's eye and waved, pushing up his glasses with his middle finger in a motion that even Winnie, immortal, supernatural, and quintessentially inhuman, recognized as a stereotypical dork move. And yet, self-consciously, she reached up and flattened out her messy, still-damp locks.

Tod had harried her ceaselessly from the moment she'd opened her bedroom door until she'd finally locked the front door behind them on the way out, hurrying her along so much that she was sure she hadn't grabbed anything they were likely to need. He'd dismissed the notion of Nolan joining their search party the moment Winnie mentioned it; despite her insistence that one more person could only help them, he'd argued determinedly against it. Who would keep him safe? Who would explain all the things his feeble mortal mind would struggle to comprehend? Who would attend to his irritatingly mortal needs, like eating and toileting?

"He's a grown man, Tod. Not a labradoodle," Winnie had responded coolly, trying to make sense of the mishmash of supplies crammed into her backpack.

Huffing and muttering under his breath, he'd rushed her out the door and down the stairs just to stand there uselessly, waiting for Nolan to appear. So, she'd slung her backpack off her shoulder and unzipped it, rummaging through its contents right down to the bottom to see if, just by chance, she'd managed to leave something useful in it, like a hairbrush perhaps, the last time she'd used it.

But just then, Nolan had rounded the corner. Whatever lay ahead of them now, she'd have to hope the contents of the bag—a pack of gum, two mini-flashlights, a half empty box of granola bars, two lukewarm water bottles, one change of clothes (two changes of underpants, of course), and, inexplicably, a deck of Uno cards held together with a cracked, ancient rubber band—would be enough to get them into the afterlife and back again.

"Winnie! Hi," Nolan said breathlessly as he approached the three of them.

"Hey, Nolan," Winnie answered, realizing for the first time how much more awkward this was about to become. Nolan had never minced words when it came to Tod: as far as he was concerned, Tod was irredeemably bad, having first caused discord among the Elementals with global climatological repercussions and subsequently having enticed Nina, Nolan's only sibling and best friend, to leave the mortal realm altogether, a situation Nolan still struggled to fully understand despite Winnie's many attempts to explain it all.

Now the two of them would not only have to meet one another in person but work together. Inwardly, Winnie groaned. From the look on Tod's face, news of Nolan's disapproval had filtered down to him one way or another, and he appraised Nolan from above, looking down on the shorter man with an expression of faint repulsion, like a CEO forced to spend a day slumming on the factory floor.

"Uh, Nolan, this is Tod," Winnie said, waving a hand vaguely toward her brother-in-law. "And this is his sister, Vita."

"Yep. Got it. Where to?"

Winnie raised her eyebrows, but if the black-haired siblings were affronted, they gave no sign of it.

"There's an entrance to the Depths close by," Tod informed them, making no move to extend a greeting of any kind to Nolan. "But, it's not exactly well-concealed. We'll have to be discreet."

"Discreet is my middle name," Winnie announced with confidence, grabbing the backpack from the concrete at her feet and swinging it up onto one shoulder with gusto.

It wasn't zipped. With a clatter, the contents of the bag scattered across the sidewalk in an arc, the Uno cards snapping through their geriatric bonds on impact and fanning out into the gutter and a wadded-up pair of clean undies landing artlessly on Nolan's left shoe.

Vita snorted in amusement. Nolan bent, hooked Winnie's underpants with one tentative finger, and held them out to her, his lips mashed together and his eyebrows creased in an expression of sympathy. Winnie snatched them off his finger and shoved them into the bag, her face burning.

The next time she undertook a perilous journey into the underworld, she'd remember not to pack underwear printed with the days of the week.

Fifteen

Several blocks—and one waspish comment from Tod about changing her middle name—later, Winnie looked up to find that they stood at the wrought-iron gates of a small cemetery that had once likely been a churchyard that had somehow survived as its church was shuttered and the city grew up around it.

"What is this place?" Nolan asked no one in particular, and no one extended the courtesy of a reply. Looking first left and then right as if a mustachioed stranger intending malice might be skulking nearby, Tod casually but determinedly passed through the gates. A moment later, looking around in the same way her brother had, Vita followed him.

Winnie looked at Nolan, who wore the perplexed look she imagined herself wearing at that moment as well. After watching Vita's retreating back for a beat, he turned to look at Winnie. She raised her eyebrows in mute appeal.

"They're a couple of kooks. Am I right?" he asked.

Winnie cocked her head to one side and grinned. "*Kooks*? Really? Am I going to have to lure you in there with a Scooby Snack?"

Nolan stared blankly at Winnie just long enough for her to cringe inwardly before he released a sound halfway between a honk and a sneeze. He followed that with a wheezy, high-pitched laugh and capped it off—to Winnie's secret delight—with a snort.

She giggled and snaked her arm around Nolan's. "Come on, Shaggy. You're finally going to see in real life what Nina and I have been trying to describe all this time."

They caught up with Tod and Vita in what seemed to be the center of the graveyard, where the ill-maintained path leading in from the gate bisected a broader and even worse-maintained path, this one curving around to either side to encircle a crumbling yet still-stately stone fountain.

Stopping and dropping Nolan's arm, she looked around. Sparse ornamental crab trees dotted the graveyard, but she heard no birds singing in their branches. And, while she could hear the city noises all around them, they seemed strangely distant. The headstones that radiated out from the point at which they stood were weather-worn and filthy. Those that stood in the sparse shade of the trees were spotted with lichen that seemed itself on the brink of demise, and the ones that canted drunkenly outside the meager protection of the trees' branches were pitted from weather and bleached to near-unreadability.

"How old is this graveyard?" she asked Tod, turning to step off the path to examine the headstones for dates. A hand on her arm, pincer-tight, startled her, and she looked up into her brother-in-law's stern face.

"Don't step off the path. I told you that we need to be discreet."

Winnie looked out through the trees, scanning the passersby on the city sidewalks. Despite the sizable pedestrian presence, no one seemed to pay any attention to the four of them. In fact, no one seemed even to notice the graveyard as they passed it.

114

"These graves are pretty old, Tod. Do you really think someone is going to come here this early on a weekday to visit the grave of someone who died a century ago? What's the point of being so discreet if there aren't any people around?"

Tod's eyes scanned the graveyard grimly, and when he answered Winnie, his voice was scarcely above a whisper. "It's not people I'm trying to avoid," he muttered.

Winnie swallowed. She scooted back to the center of the pathway, a little closer to Nolan, who was peering into the fountain, apparently oblivious to the conversation happening behind him.

"Is this how we're getting to…getting where we're going?" he asked. Winnie joined Nolan, looking down at the cracked basin. The fountain had likely once been lovely. Its basin was wide enough for even Tod to lie comfortably spread out in, and from its center rose a single pillar topped by a stone woman. Her head was scarved, and her upturned face was eerily eyeless. One hand reached out toward the two onlookers; the other clutched a shallow bowl that tipped precariously in her grasp. Long-dry stains showed where water once ran over the edge of the bowl, dropping in a perpetual stream into the great basin below.

Winnie studied the woman's face uncomfortably. Despite the smooth bulges of her unseeing eyes, her face still managed to convey despair. Winnie shivered.

"I guess? I don't know how he gets back and forth. When I came up with him after Nina and I went looking for Verna, we came out through the same place we'd gone in." Nolan looked at her blankly. "In the tunnels under my dad's shop," she filled in.

"Gotcha," Nolan responded, and Winnie realized his conversations with Nina probably focused on what she was doing now rather than on the adventure she'd gone on with Winnie. Illogically, Winnie felt a twinge of sadness at that thought. But after all, why would they talk about her when Nina had so much going on?

Tod, who had continued to scan the graveyard suspiciously, finally joined Winnie and Nolan beside the fountain, and Vita, apparently sensing it was time for something to get underway, fell in beside her brother.

"What now, Tod?" Winnie asked.

"Your dad found a way into the Depths using his element, Winnie, but I don't normally pass back and forth the way you did. We're going in through water. I've used the pool here many times, and it's mostly been safe, so I don't think we'll have any trouble."

Nolan's head shot up and he said, "*Mostly* safe?" at exactly the same time Winnie said skeptically, "Water?" She glanced at Nolan when she'd processed what he'd said and then looked back at Tod.

"Strike that. Forget about the water. I want to know what you mean by 'mostly safe' too," she said with dignity.

Tod drew breath to answer, but it was Vita who spoke. "He means this door isn't heavily guarded by Nights," she said.

"Ah-ha," Nolan said, pushing up his glasses. The motion reminded Winnie of Nina, and it struck her how urgent this was for Nolan. She scolded herself about being mindful of just how much he stood to lose if they didn't figure out exactly what was going on in the Depths.

Nolan was peering at Vita.

"Yes, that explains...," he paused, staring off hazily as he considered. "Actually," he continued with more verve, "that explains nothing at all. What knights are we talking about?"

Tod piped up in response, "That's *Nights* with an *n*, not a *k*. This isn't Camelot," he added snidely. Rolling his eyes at Nolan's blank look, he went on, "They're liminal beings that safeguard the portals between realms, existing as entities both other and not, excluded from life and shunned by death to maintain their vim."

Nolan gaped at Tod, and when he turned to give Winnie a searching look, she shrugged and responded, "Search me. All I'm picturing is Monty Python."

"Ni!" Nolan yelped, and Winnie guffawed, elbowing him in the stomach good-naturedly. Vita narrowed her eyes and watched as the two of them snickered privately, their cheeks reddening when they realized neither she nor her brother shared their amusement.

Nolan cleared his throat awkwardly, apparently fighting the urge to affect a British accent. "Right. So...if I'm hearing you correctly then...What you seem to be saying is..."

Tod rolled his eyes again, and heaved the type of sigh normally reserved for a teenager being asked to bear the weight of the world by hefting a laundry basket down the stairs. "They're big, supernatural monsters that live in the Liminus between life and death. They keep dead stuff in the Depths and live stuff out of it," he said.

Nolan's still-pink cheeks blanched. "Ah."

"Exactly," Tod asserted, and Winnie bristled at how much he seemed to enjoy Nolan's discomfort.

"Well," Winnie interjected briskly. "That's all fine. But I don't see how this is going to work. Have you looked into this fountain, Tod? It's bone dry."

"Okay...," Tod let the word trail off as if he wasn't entirely sure what she was getting at. "I'm not entirely sure what you're getting at," he said.

"How are we supposed to use this fountain to get into the Depths if there's no water in it? That's what I'm getting at," Winnie answered.

Tod squeezed the bridge of his nose with his thumb and forefinger, the international sign for *I am quite literally the only intelligent person within a six-mile radius*. Winnie, who was guilty of making that same gesture on more than one occasion and knew exactly what it meant, began a long, slow inhalation, one that would give her a few seconds to articulate her opinion of that expression, the man making it, and the particular piece of anatomy he was welcome to introduce his fountain to when Vita spoke up.

"The fountain isn't the portal, Winnie," she said, and Winnie was pleasantly surprised to find that her tone was kind rather than derisive.

"Oh."

"Follow me," Tod commanded. He turned and headed up a path that branched away from the fountain, his long strides covering the ground with rapid familiarity. Vita, tall like her brother, kept up without complaint, which left Winnie and Nolan all but jogging after them.

Tod pulled up short before a stunted crab tree, one branch canting off bizarrely, the lone living holdout on an otherwise shriveled and leafless crown. Beneath the solitary leafy branch sat a concrete bench and a moldy birdbath, a skimpy puddle of scummy water motionless in its basin. The path ran parallel to the bench before winding away through the graves.

"This is it," said Tod.

"This is what?" asked Nolan, studying the bench skeptically.

"This is the door. I'll open it and go through first. You three follow me closely. We walk straight once we pass through."

"Wait, what? Through what? Follow you where?" Nolan's voice had risen an octave, and Winnie sensed his burgeoning panic.

Apparently, so did Vita. She turned to Nolan and put her hand on his shoulder. Winnie watched his profile as his expression changed minutely from anxious anger to contentment.

"It's going to be fine, Nolan." Her voice sent a sensation like dripping hot fudge down Winnie's spine.

"Okay. Sure. Lead on, Tod," Nolan said agreeably. Winnie studied his face as he turned back to watch Tod. Vita certainly had impressive skills.

Movement at the bench drew Winnie's attention. Tod had climbed up onto it with two quick scissors of his long legs. He faced the birdbath, balancing at the very end of the bench so that he could look directly down into its murky basin. Bending forward, he inserted one long, bony finger into the bath and touched the center of the water. Mosquitos lifted up from the edges of the puddle when the ripples he caused reached the edge.

"Gross," said Winnie helpfully.

He scowled at her once, briefly, before closing his eyes, breathing deeply, and exhaling a single, inaudible word.

Winnie watched the water in the birdbath. It trembled around his finger, and when he began to withdraw it, the water seemed to climb and swirl around his pale digit. It rose perhaps six inches before pulling away from Tod's finger. He stood upright and watched as the water spun in an ever-widening hoop, growing like a water spout in reverse until the rotating, glistening funnel dwarfed the decrepit birdbath that had birthed it.

Nolan's mouth hung open. Either Vita's effect had worn off already or his genuine shock at what he was seeing had overpowered it. Discreetly, Winnie raised a hand to ease his jaw closed.

Snapping out of his trance, Nolan turned to look at her. "This isn't possible. It's not physically possible for that...*that* to have come out of there. There wasn't enough water in there!" His voice was barely above a whisper.

"Honey, water is life," Vita answered him, her dark eyes glued to the dancing, glittering funnel. "Water is

120

everywhere. Now, you're really seeing it for the first time."

Nolan didn't respond, and Winnie saw why. With a final look at his sister, Tod nodded sharply, raised one leg, and stepped forward into the cyclone. Leaning forward, he picked his other foot up off the bench and stood in the water, his feet disappearing behind its rushing ridge. Then, like a man descending a circular stairway, he began walking down into the water, each step taking him down incrementally until his head disappeared below the funnel's rim.

Vita, clearly less enthralled by the spectacle of a grown man disappearing into a birdbath than either Nolan or Winnie, was already climbing onto the bench, preparing to follow her brother. But when she looked back to herd the stragglers into formation, she groaned.

Winnie tore her eyes from the watery door and glanced at Vita. "What's wrong?" she asked.

"Your boyfriend just made this a whole lot harder," Vita said, the ice from the previous night's shenanigans back in her voice.

"Who did what now?" Winnie asked.

Verna put her hands on her hips and jerked her chin to Winnie's right. "What was the one thing Tod told you two *not* to do?"

Winnie pondered. "Not to step off the path? But we didn't...," she trailed off, turning, stiff as a board, to look behind her.

Nolan looked at her, wide-eyed, before dropping his gaze to the grass under his feet. Meeting her eyes again, he grimaced sheepishly.

Winnie sighed. "Oh…elderberries," she cursed.

Sixteen

Reaching out and grabbing Nolan's forearm to yank him back onto the path, Winnie directed her next question at Vita.

"What do we do now?"

Nolan peered around the cemetery as if skeletal arms might erupt from the ground around them at any second. None did.

Vita hadn't climbed down from the bench. "We do exactly what Tod told us to do. We walk straight through as quickly as we can."

"But then why—" Nolan began, but Vita cut him off with a piercing glance.

"We walk straight through, I said. Nothing I tell you now is going to make this easier. So just stay close to me and head straight for the door." Her gaze softened as she said, "Just...don't look to the left or right, okay? Don't look around at all. Hopefully, we'll see the light under the door as soon as we enter the Liminus. When you see it, just walk straight to it."

Nolan glanced nervously at Winnie. "What's in there, Winnie?" he asked.

Winnie studied Vita's face, wondering if she was imagining the beseeching tension around her eyes.

In a flash, she made up her mind. "Nothing we can't handle, Nolan." She flashed him a smile and clutched his arm at the elbow, urging him toward the bench. "It'll be fine, okay? You just follow Vita, and I'll be right behind you."

Nolan balked. "Behind me? No, no. You should follow Vita. I'll bring up the rear."

"That's very kind of you, but I'd feel better knowing you're safe between Vita and me," Winnie responded.

Nolan adjusted his glasses, and smiled tightly. "Really, Winnie, I insist—"

"Shut up, Galahad," Vita broke in. "While your chivalry is appreciated, you're human, which means your frail, mortal vessel can be killed by a carrot. So, I'll be leading, and Winnie will be our rear guard. Got it?" She didn't bother waiting for a response before turning back to the swirling cyclone and placing one foot inside.

With an apologetic shrug, Winnie pushed Nolan forward. He scrambled up onto the bench and peered down into the water funnel. Standing behind him, Winnie followed his gaze.

Tod's circular descent now made sense. Translucent, watery steps lined the waterspout, descending in an impossible spiral into darkness. Vita's head and shoulders, the only parts of her still above the waterline, turned toward them, and she hissed, "Come on!"

Winnie poked Nolan in the ribs; he drew a deep breath, stuck one leg out comically, and tipped forward. When his foot landed safely on a step, he turned to look at Winnie.

"I did it!" he exclaimed gleefully.

Winnie resisted the urge to pat him on the head and instead smiled encouragingly. He pulled his other leg over the water's rim and studied his feet. Though he stood on moving water, his shoes remained dry.

Gingerly, he took a step, and when that proved sturdy, he carried on, his upper half disappearing like the siblings' had. When he'd cleared enough space, Winnie followed, scrambling over the edge with one last look at the mortal world they were leaving behind.

Several disorienting minutes passed in which Winnie found herself grasping repeatedly for a connection to Nolan's form, which seemed to be slipping away. Her foot found its way to each step reliably, but Nolan seemed to slip in and out of sight as he descended the stairs below her. Fearful of losing him, she avoided looking up at the aperture they'd passed through, but finally she could resist no longer, and she peered up through the circular opening at the measly pink flowers of the ornamental crab beneath which the birdbath sat.

Satisfied with a quick glance, she peered back down through the watery steps to locate Nolan. The light was dimming rapidly, and she found herself beginning to worry that it would run out completely before they'd reached the bottom. What would happen if the three of them made it to a landing shrouded in darkness and struck out in three different directions.

Her opportunity to worry about that was cut short when she put out a foot to find the next step and discovered instead that she'd come to the end of the stairway. The jolt of unexpected floor under her foot knocked her off balance, and she flung her arms out reactively. They made contact with something fleshy.

Winnie shrieked, though the sound seemed muffled and flat. Her shriek was paired with Nolan's muted exclamation.

"Youch! Damn, Winnie," she heard him say. This was followed by the hissing sound of breath being drawn in through a grimace.

"Sorry!" she breathed. "Did I hit you?"

"You punched me in the ear."

"I'm really sorry, but I didn't 'punch' you. I threw out my hands, and your ear just happened to be in the way."

"Are you sure about that? I'm just saying that it definitely felt like a punch."

Winnie bristled. "Well, it wasn't. But it's becoming increasingly possible that next time, it will be."

"Winnie, I really don't think—"

"Shut up, both of you," came a voice out of the darkness.

"Vita?" Winnie asked stupidly, and she heard the snort she knew she deserved from the dark space to her left.

"Brilliant deduction, Einstein," Vita hissed. "Now put your hand on my shoulder, Nolan. We need to move fast and stay silent."

There was a shuffling sound in the dark, and then a few beats of silence.

"Nolan?"

"What?"

"That's not my shoulder."

This was followed by a yelp, after which Winnie snickered. She could practically hear Nolan blushing.

When the three of them had finally attached themselves to one another, hands to shoulders, they began to move. Winnie felt her senses on high alert, and she craned to the left and right to see around where she thought Vita must be ahead of her, searching for the pinprick of light she remembered from her last journey through this in-between place.

Liminus, she reminded herself. *It has a name. This place isn't just a dark space between two worlds; it's a world of its own. And it's inhabited.* The thought made her shiver.

When she'd gone through the first time with Nina, the excitement of the experience had overshadowed any feelings of dread; she and Nina had picked out the pinprick of light in the dark depths immediately upon passing through the door Pete had opened for them, and Winnie hadn't even considered whether or not she should be afraid. Later, Tod led them back out, his sure footing and her joy at having Verna back had distracted her once again. Had Tod cautioned them then to stay close? To move quickly? She hadn't paid attention, and she certainly hadn't given any thought to the space they passed through or what might be alerted to their presence there.

In fact, she'd gone through so quickly both times that she hadn't even needed the…

"Flashlight!" she chirruped, and two answering voices grunted in surprise. "You guys, I totally forgot I have a flashlight!"

Without taking her hand off Nolan's shoulder, she popped her other arm out of the pack's strap and tilted it so that it hung off the crook of her shoulder. She dug around in the pack with her free hand. In the background, Vita was hissing in a whisper, raising some kind of objection. Winnie's fingers touched cool metal, and she snatched out the mini torch and clicked it on, lighting her face from below like a campfire storyteller.

"What are you saying, Vita? I wasn't listening."

Vita pinched the bridge of her nose in exactly the same way her brother had back in the cemetery. "I was saying, Winnie, that it's better if you don't turn on a light in here," she explained in a whisper. "For one thing, it's going to make it harder to see the light from the door."

"Oh," Winnie answered, feeling sheepish. "What's the second thing?"

"The second thing is that you've just made us very, very visible."

"Visible to what?" Nolan's voice quavered just the tiniest bit, and Winnie squeezed his shoulder a little tighter.

They were on the move once again, Winnie clinging to Nolan who clung, in turn, to Vita. He'd nearly lost his grip on Vita's shoulder when she'd started walking again after the flashlight fiasco, so he'd tightened his hold on her; their height difference meant he had to walk closer than either of them preferred in order to reach her shoulder, and his toe frequently clipped her heel so that the silence in which they walked, a heavy, muffled stillness, was frequently punctuated by him hissing apologies in a carrying stage whisper and Vita hissing *shhh!* right back.

If Winnie had been in a better place—both physically and psychologically—she would have rolled her eyes at this two-man act, but she was too busy being terrified of the cryptic scolding Vita had delivered when she'd turned on her flashlight.

After the reprimand, Winnie had hastily clicked off the light, but Vita had pawed at her in the disorienting blackness that followed, insisting she turn it back on and claiming the damage was done: she'd already announced their presence, Vita had told her, so she should put the torch to good use by keep an eye out for anything approaching from the rear.

So, now they moved through the darkness in a state of unhappy compromise. Nolan's left hand clutched Winnie's, allowing her to point the flashlight behind them and scan left and right for…anything.

She swallowed and tried to murmur over one shoulder while her eyes continued moving around behind them.

"It wasn't like this when Nina and I went through, Vita. It didn't take this long to find the other door. Are you sure we're going the right way?"

Perhaps it was a trick of her imagination, but she thought she heard the sound of an impatient sigh from the front of the line.

"You went through a different door. Consider yourself lucky it happened to be one with a straight shot to the other side. And no, I'm not sure we're going the right way. We'd be better off if Nolan hadn't gotten us separated from Tod. Now shut up."

Winnie opened her mouth to defend Nolan but decided she probably shouldn't. She resumed her ceaseless scanning. The flashlight beam hardly penetrated the darkness at all; it unsettled her how, rather than illuminating their surroundings, it only defined them, creating a barrier, like headlights bouncing off fog rather than penetrating it. It seemed the dark was communicating a clear, villainous message: this is the boundary of what's knowable to you, and all else that lies beyond it is unknowable.

Except that she did know what lay beyond that boundary. Or at least she had a name for it.

Risking Vita's continued ire, she craned her neck around again and whispered, "Vita, what exactly are Nights?"

There was a pause before Vita responded, and when she did, her tone lacked the irritation Winnie had anticipated.

"They're what Tod described," she said solemnly.

"Tod called them 'monsters.' But what are they really? Why do they exist?"

"We shouldn't be talking about this now," Vita responded. "We shouldn't be talking at all."

"Right. Yes, I understand," Winnie answered. But a beat later, she spoke again. "But the reason I'm asking now is because I'm on lookout duty, and I really don't know what I'm looking for…"

Vita stopped so suddenly that Nolan slammed into her back, and Winnie stepped down hard on his heel, making him grunt in pain.

"Stop talking, Winnie," Vita spat quietly but dangerously. "Just stop. Anything you see in that light is something we don't want to deal with, so if you see *anything*, hold as tight as you can to Nolan's hand and start running in the opposite direction. Got it?"

Winnie nodded doltishly and then squeaked in mousy agreement when she remembered Vita couldn't see her head moving.

They began to walk again, and Winnie resumed her reconnaissance.

The longer they walked and the more she scanned, the harder it became to feel oriented in the darkness. Did Vita know which direction they were headed? Did directions even exist here? She thought back to the first time she'd looked out over the expanse of the Depths after she and Nina had passed through the door they'd found in the darkness. She remembered how land had spread out in all directions, how mountains, forests, and oceans seemed to exist, illogically, side-by-side. It had been beautiful and breathtaking and…uncanny.

Uncanny indeed. She'd recognized everything she'd seen; after all, she'd been alive a long time and had seen much. But though the Depths were familiar, they weren't quite right. She remembered how she and Nina had looked out over the same landscape but couldn't identify the same structures. And she remembered turning to take it all in, returning to the position she'd started from, and finding that what she was sure she remembered being there was there no longer.

Because it *wasn't* there any longer; in fact, it wasn't there at all. Because it wasn't really real...not in the way the world she inhabited was real, at least. Did directions exist there? Did distance? She already knew time was different there: she and Nina had been gone only hours, but whole weeks had stretched away back among the living. If Vita was walking in what she thought was a straight line, did that mean it actually was straight? What if they were walking in circles? What if they just kept walking like this...forever? What if, here in the liminal darkness, time didn't exist at all and they—

Something shifted at the edge of the flashlight's beam. Winnie jerked the light back in the direction she thought she'd seen movement, and the sudden motion alerted Vita and Nolan. All three of them froze.

"Winnie," Nolan whispered beside her. "Did you see something?"

Unspeaking, Winnie moved the flashlight as steadily as her shaking hand permitted around the area. She'd gotten distracted by her spiraling thoughts, she knew. Could it have been just her mind playing tricks?

When several beats of silent searching revealed nothing, she breathed out slowly, though she hadn't realized she was holding her breath.

"No," she croaked. Her voice was weaker than she would have liked, and an uncomfortable feeling like ice water suffused her hands and feet while a hot flush warmed her face. She had passed out of feeling and into mortal terror. Immortal terror, at least. But there was no sign of movement.

She said again, slightly steadier, "No. No, I...don't think so."

Without a word, Vita began walking again, and Winnie loosened her grip on Nolan's hand. It must have been uncomfortably tight.

She kept her light trained off to the left, scanning the area with laser focus. As the minutes passed and nothing happened, she felt the ice water in her extremities drain off. It had been nothing.

Breathing deeply as her heart rate slowed, she resumed the arcing motion she'd been using, swinging the light back around to the right.

"Vita." She said quietly, no longer bothering to whisper.

"What now?" Vita's tone was irritated once more, and her steps didn't pause.

Winnie swallowed once, hard. "Run."

Seventeen

Vita's reaction time was so robust, so healthy, that no more than a second could have elapsed between Winnie's command and the tug on her hand that pulled her from her frozen, panicked torpor into breathless flight. But for Winnie, that second seemed to stretch out into a terrifying eternity.

The thing in her flashlight beam wasn't simply black. Blackness, like the blackness that surrounded them in this place between doors, was comprehensible. She had spent lots of time underground in her lifetime: her father's penchant for tunneling and mining provided endless opportunities for experiencing true total darkness, the utter absence of light that could be achieved only in places buried beneath the earth.

But the Night...it wasn't blackness or darkness. Winnie studied it without blinking as it consumed the flashlight's beam, and she knew without having to search for the word exactly what she was looking at.

The Night was absence. It was removal. It was void.

And it was inside of her.

When Nolan's hand tugged her forward, her feet began to move, but no part of her mind seemed to be sending them the command to do so. Nolan's grip, despite his diminutive size, was intense and unwavering; if it had been even the smallest bit less so, she might have slackened her grasp and let her hand fall away from his.

Instead, she cast the now wildly-bouncing light beam back over her shoulder as they ran because she

134

was the lookout, and it was her job to know whether or not an enemy was attacking from the rear. That had been Vita's command. The light swung in wild bobs that she struggled to control.

But really, they should stop, she realized, because she wasn't a very good lookout if she couldn't *look out* at the Night. If she couldn't look *into* the Night. They should definitely stop.

She opened her mouth to shout out to Vita that they could stop running. The Night wasn't something to fear: it was the natural order of all things. It was the end of existing, and all things had to pass out of existence.

Before she had a chance to speak, Vita yelled back over her shoulder, "Don't look at it, Winnie! Don't look into it! You can't handle what you'll see there!"

Nolan let out a frightened whimper that cut off abruptly as he drew in a breath. They were running flat out, their gaits wonky and misaligned as they fought to avoid tripping themselves or one another.

Winnie dropped the flashlight to her side and fought the urge to search behind them, but her resistance lasted only the span of a few steps before she raised it once again and fought to see the Night.

It was to her left now, and it moved along beside her effortlessly, flowing like water, its intense absence making the darkness around it feel as innocent and harmless as the gloaming. Winnie fought to keep the light trained on its form.

Except…it had no form: it wasn't a monster in the way the level threes, the profoundly and inherently bad essences who had tried to kill her and Nina on their last visit to the Depths, had been monsters. It wasn't like the monsters from the beginning of the world that her parents had told her and her sisters bedtime stories about...

Her parents...Her sisters...

Renata. With an effort that was physically painful, Winnie tore her attention from the Night. She squeezed Nolan's hand and clicked off the flashlight, squinting in the sudden darkness to search for the pinprick of light that would bring her closer to Ren.

When the light snapped off, a sweeping roar sounded around them, and in spite of her remembered resolve to find her niece, Winnie cried out in fear. The sound grew and changed, swirling around them in a mind-numbing shriek, assaulting them first from one side and then from another. Vaguely, she realized Vita was screaming, the sound nearly drowned out by the wailing screeches that enveloped them.

"Scream!" Vita broke off her own cries to command Winnie and Nolan. "Scream to keep the sound out! Don't let them in!" She resumed her own screaming, and Winnie and Nolan joined their voices to hers, shrieking and gasping as they struggled to keep running. Winnie's lungs and throat burned. Her legs and back resisted the prolonged effort of staying upright, connected to Nolan, and out of his and Vita's way.

But even with so much terror and pain to distract her, her mind managed to tease out one word from Vita's directive: *them.*

The Night wasn't screaming from all sides: Nights on all sides were screaming to one another.

Winnie had never hunted an animal, but she knew exactly what the Nights were doing to them nonetheless.

To her right, Nolan's screams suddenly changed, and to her horror, she felt him change direction, not to the left or to the right, but *up*. Vita's screams cut off as well, and Winnie felt a hand clutch at the front of her clothes in the darkness. She dropped the flashlight and grabbed the hand instead, recognizing the large, strong hand, so different from the other one she still held firmly, as Vita's. A reassuring warmth spread up her arm, and Winnie squeezed Vita's hand in appreciation.

"Winnie!" Vita yelled to her through the grating howls around them. "I lost him! He let go! Do you still have Nolan? Winnie, do you have him?" The desperation in Vita's voice temporarily robbed Winnie of speech.

"I have him! Yes! I have him!" Nolan was an invisible, silent weight at the end of her arm, but she held tighter still.

"Don't let him go, Winnie!" Vita screamed again. "Don't let them take him!"

They had slowed as they fought to reorganize, and they slowed further as the pull of Nolan's grasp increased. Winnie barked out a wheezing whimper. She was going to lose him. She wouldn't be able to keep him from the Nights.

Her grasp was loosening, fatigue taking its toll. She groaned with the effort of running and pulling and fighting, but there was only so much her body could take. A fledgling impulse to use her power sparked for a moment within her, but she quashed it just as quickly. She needed focus and energy to direct her element, and there was no way to muster those things now and no materials at hand to harness even if she could manage it.

Tears welled in her eyes, angry, bitter tears at the thought that this would be the destruction of not just her and Vita, powerful though they were, but of Nolan as well, and of Ren's and Nina's hope.

Tears streamed back from her eyes, blurring the nothingness before her, blurring the dot of light in the distance into a glittery, insubstantial star.

Winnie gasped. "Vita!"

"I know!" Vita screamed back. "I see it! Don't slow down! Just run!"

And Winnie did. She had no strength left, no endurance. And yet she felt her grip on Nolan's hand tighten as she pulled him along behind them like the meatiest balloon in history. Running side by side, hand in hand, the two women moved as one, determination and the slowly-growing glint in the distance driving them on.

Tod had just stepped through the doorway and was turning to see why the others were taking so long to come through behind him when the crushing darkness split, and three rampaging forms plowed into him at full speed. He tumbled back on his scrawny rear, his sister's momentum somersaulting her painfully over his face and onto the parched, cracked dirt surrounding the door. Winnie scrambled over his supine form next, managing to keep her footing better than Vita had but consequently stepping on several soft and vulnerable anatomical structures as she stumbled over him. She collapsed somewhere between him and Vita.

Nolan, apparently having the least forward momentum, flew through the door behind Winnie and landed on Tod's now-tender form with a heavy thud, like a trash bag full of thawed chicken parts thrown from a moving vehicle.

For a moment, none of the four moved, and the sounds of gasps, pants, and wheezes slowly gave way to a single wry chuckle, courtesy of Vita.

Winnie scrambled on hands and knees over to Nolan's body, cringing slightly at discovering his face pressed against the bit of Tod's abdomen visible between his disheveled shirt and his waistband. Tod, still sprawled on his back, picked himself up on his elbows to glare thunderously at the top of Nolan's head.

"Nolan?" she said gingerly. "Nolan, can you hear me?"

Nolan opened his eyes and looked woozily at Winnie's face and then down into Tod's bellybutton. Jerking back in surprise, he looked directly into Tod's eyes.

"Get. Off. Me."

Nolan's arms and legs flailed around haphazardly as he maneuvered himself groggily off the other man. Winnie offered what assistance she could, but exhaustion prevented her from helping much, and Tod finally lost patience and rolled out from under them both. Silently thankful for the now uninhabited patch of land in front of her, Winnie let go of Nolan and flopped down on it, closing her eyes and focusing on not having to do anything but breathe and hurt.

"What the hell were you idiots doing?" Tod growled, straightening his clothes with what little dignity he could muster and turning on his still-supine sister.

"Outrunning the Nights," she managed.

"Nights? What Nights? I didn't see anything when I came through. They shouldn't even have known we were coming through the door..." His words trailed off as he turned to look at the other two recumbent figures. "Oh, let me guess," he said, his voice dripping sarcasm. "One of you managed to do the one thing I told you not to?"

Nolan gallantly raised a single finger from where he'd—following Winnie's lead—collapsed beside her.

"Oops," he said breathlessly.

Tod swiped a bony hand over his long face, muttering something Winnie didn't catch but which sounded less than complimentary.

Beside her, Winnie heard Nolan sit up. "Hey, did you find anything out while you were waiting?"

"What do you mean, *while I was waiting*? I just got here too, remember?" Tod's tone suggested he wasn't ready to forgive Nolan for the Night debacle yet.

Nolan didn't respond, and Winnie propped herself up on her elbows, turning to him. "Time moves differently here, remember?"

Nolan stared at her blankly.

"Like…slower," she added.

"Winnie, what…?" Nolan's voice trailed off, and his brow furrowed in concern.

She sat up quickly, regretted it, closed her eyes again for a moment as her head swam, and then scrubbed her face with her hands.

Reaching out a comforting hand, she patted Nolan's shoulder. "Don't worry. It works in our favor if Ren and Nina are here and in trouble…"

"No, that's not…"

"We'll find them, Nolan." After having just survived a terrifying ordeal, Winnie felt pretty pleased with herself for keeping it together so effectively.

Go me! she thought.

"No, Winnie, stop talking for a minute. I'm not asking about the time," Nolan insisted. "I'm asking about your eyes."

Winnie drew back. "My eyes? What about them?"

"Here," he said, fumbling in his pocket for his cell. He tapped the screen a few times and turned it around to show her. "Look."

She took the phone, dread bottoming out her stomach. She gazed at the screen where the selfie camera showed her an image of her own face.

Her irises were completely white.

Eighteen

"The hell...?" Winnie murmured, trying in vain to simultaneously look directly at the camera to get the best view of her eyes and at the screen where her face was displayed. She wasn't fast enough. She could feel warm breath and glanced up to see Nolan inspecting her like a scientist analyzing an intriguing specimen.

"Can you see?" Nolan asked, and despite her concern over what she was seeing in the phone, she warmed at the concern in his voice

"I doubt she'd be studying herself like that if she couldn't see," Vita said unhelpfully from behind Winnie. Tod snorted in response, but when Winnie turned to shoot him a quelling look, the smirk dropped from his face, and he stepped closer to where she sat.

Sensing her brother's changed mood, Vita sat up suddenly, her brown eyes taking in Tod's stance and shifting briskly to the point of his focus: Winnie's face.

She climbed to her feet without blinking, a low whistle escaping from between her teeth.

Winnie felt her face burn, and she turned her back on the looky-loos, staring wide-eyed into the phone's front camera and snapping off a series of selfies. She opened the photos and began flipping through them furiously, searching for any sign of the blue eyes she was so accustomed to seeing when she looked in the mirror.

But they weren't there. All that stared out at her from photo after photo were deep black pupils inside hazy, pearlescent irises. Only a faint, bluish tint around their edges differentiated the irises from the sclera.

Winnie didn't realize the siblings had moved to stand over her until one of them moved, and when she looked up, the brightness of their surroundings seemed piercing. She shut her eyes, rubbing at them furiously as they burned and watered.

"Take these," Nolan said, pulling sunglasses from a pocket in his cargo pants and handing them to Winnie. "They're prescription, but it's not that strong. Your eyes might be more sensitive to light now."

"How come?" She peeked out at him through squinted eyes and accepted the sunglasses gratefully.

"No melanin."

"Well, where did it go?" Winnie heard the shrillness in her voice, but at the moment she didn't care that she was whining. She turned to look up at Tod, who felt too close and too tall standing over her the way he was.

His looming bulk suddenly infuriated her. "Where's my melanin, Tod? What did those things do to me?" she demanded.

Tod didn't answer but rather dropped to one knee and motioned for her to remove the glasses again. She did so grudgingly, and he looked from one eye to the other.

"Stop blinking," he told her, but she only sighed and blinked more as her eyes began watering again.

He stood and looked at Vita, who was turned away from them, scanning the middle-distance. A look passed over his face that Winnie, even with the sunglasses now shielding her eyes once more, couldn't quite read. Was he waiting for her to chime in with an answer? Or was he wondering something else altogether?

He looked back down at her. "I don't know," he finally said. "You shouldn't have looked at the Night. They aren't...things people normally look at."

Winnie pursed her lips. "Super helpful, thanks," she muttered under her breath as she climbed painfully to her feet. If they ever got out of this mess, she was going to take the world's longest shower. Right after she paid a visit to her ophthalmologist, of course.

She joined Nolan, who had also turned his back to the small group and was staring out around them. Having come through a different door previously, Winnie wasn't surprised to discover that the view from this door was entirely different from the one she'd first seen with Nina.

They seemed to be in the bottom of a caldera, its great, concave sides curving up and away from them in three directions as if they stood in the bottom of a bowl. A tipped bowl, Winnie discovered as she rotated slowly to take in the view. The highest face of the crater appeared from where they stood at the bottom to be just a sheer rock face, but the opposite crater wall rose very little, and beyond it, she could see land stretching into the cloud-shrouded distance.

She looked behind them. Like the previous door she'd used, the one they'd just come through had vanished.

Nolan whispered from beside her, "Are we on the top of a mountain? Or at the bottom of a crater?"

"Yes," Winnie answered.

Nolan looked at her. "That...We can't...But..."

"Yeah, I know. Just don't think about it too hard. That's what I do."

Nolan scrutinized her, apparently trying to wait out the joke. Winnie sniffed once and pushed her glasses up her nose.

Finally, he shrugged. Looking over her shoulder, he said, "I suppose you're also going to tell me there isn't really an alpaca spying on us over there, right?"

Winnie frowned and turned to follow his gaze. At the crest of the caldera, a single woolly ungulate stood watching them.

"Uhh..."

"We're not being spied on by an alpaca..." Vita filled in, her voice trailing off meaningfully.

The three of them watched the creature watching them. It crept a few steps closer and did indeed seem to be craning its substantial neck to hear them better. Winnie felt her eyebrow rise as she returned its uncanny attention.

Nolan broke the awkward silence with an equally awkward snort.

"Well, that's a relief. I thought maybe that trip through the birdbath had shaken something loose up here." He smiled at Winnie and tapped his head self-deprecatingly. He paused before adding, *sotto voce*, "Sorry, Vita, but just to clarify, are you saying that thing's not an alpaca? Or that it's not spying on us?"

"Both," Tod's voice cut in behind them. Then he called the creature over in a tone Winnie hadn't heard him use since they'd last been in the Depths. "Come closer and state your business."

The ruminant—whatever it was—leaped into movement, jogging haphazardly down the crater wall, kicking up loose sand and small rocks that tumbled down the decline ahead of it like a dust avalanche.

When it finally reached them, it stopped abruptly, sneezed two convulsive, phlegmy sneezes, and then opened its mouth.

Winnie knew practically nothing about alpacas. Llamas? Either one. In fact, what she knew about ungulates in general was fairly slim. She certainly had no familiarity with the sounds they typically made. But she knew for certain, when the creature before them began to make a noise, that it wasn't the right kind of noise at all.

"I'm certainly pleased to see you, I don't mind saying," it told them, speaking to Tod but glancing around at the other three newcomers with a look that could only be described as camelid relief.

"This isn't a thing…," Winnie heard Nolan whisper forlornly. She reached out to pat him consolingly but, unable to take her eyes off the talking…whatever, she missed his arm entirely and swatted at the air a few times before giving up and letting her hand fall limply back to her side.

"Abel told me he felt you come through, and he sent me to find you, but I wasn't sure I'd find the right place…," the creature babbled on, but Winnie lost the thread of what it was saying because its voice was so preposterous and unexpected. It bleated out the words in hot, short breaths; despite never once in her long life wondering what alpacas would sound like if they could speak, she felt strongly that this creature didn't sound right at all. It sounded more like a…

"Goat," Nolan whispered. "It sounds like a goat."

"Get out!" Winnie shrieked good-naturedly. She whacked Nolan on the chest, laughing. "That's exactly what I was thinking!"

Half of Nolan's mouth pulled up in a grin, and he rubbed the spot on his chest where she'd smacked him. Winnie grinned back…until Vita caught her eye over Nolan's shoulder with a look that said she was on the verge of pulling the car over and *coming back there.*

Winnie cleared her throat and croaked out a tiny apology before looking back expectantly at the creature.

"Go on," Tod invited.

"Yes, as I was saying," it said, casting a haughty look in Winnie's direction. She squinted behind her borrowed sunglasses, pondering how this animal managed to pull off such a dismissive gesture without eyebrows.

"Abel is detained; he's taking orders from a truly odious troglodyte of a man." Winnie caught a telling look pass between Vita and Tod. "He's no longer permitted to leave the wraith compound."

"How did he get word to you, then?" Suspicion laced Tod's voice.

The animal puffed up its chest proudly. "When that…individual stormed in and took over, I wisely kept shtum." It curled its fleshy lips around the word *individual* as if saying it tasted like spoiled milk.

Winnie frowned. How unpleasant would a person have to be to disgust a creature that regurgitated its food for re-chewing?

"Abel is one of the few wraiths who has ever cared to find out whether I'm more than just a lowly llama, so I can pass unnoticed in all the open-air areas of the compound. He simply found me, ostensibly to feed me and clean up my…well, to feed me, and then he slipped me the intel that you'd come through and sent me to get you. We should go straight back there now so that you can finally sort this mess out and—" He broke off abruptly in response to Vita's raised hand and weighty glare.

"Hold up, donkey. You haven't quite explained why we need to leave the swamp with you yet," she said.

Winnie bit her tongue as hard as she could to stop herself from snorting.

The llama—Winnie chanted this to herself several times to commit it to memory—drew itself up to its full height and peered imperiously down its long, horsey snout at Vita.

"I beg your pardon," he intoned with all the gravity his bleating, wheezing voice allowed. "I am a llama, madam. I'm no donkey. And what's more, I have a name. If you cannot extend me the courtesy of identifying my species correctly, at least attempt to remember my name. It's Gerald." Nolan raised a finger as if to ask a question, but Gerald was on a tear and continued as if he hadn't noticed.

"*Donkey*," Gerald orgled dismissively. "I'll have you know that we *L. glama* are majestic, regal, and proud."

Having delivered this pronouncement, Gerald belched audibly and regurgitated his cud, his brown eyes glazing over in contentment as he rechewed a previous meal.

The four non-pseudoruminants watched this process with voyeuristic fascination. A rustling beside her broke the spell, and she turned to see Nolan peeling back the wrapper on a jerky stick.

"What?" he said in response to her greenish complexion. "All that chewing reminded me I'm hungry."

Nineteen

It took what felt like hours to scramble up the side of the caldera after Gerald. Tod set his jaw and carried on as if his supervisor were taking notes. Similarly, Vita kept her eyes trained on the path before her, never once raising her head or speaking to the others. Gerald picked his way clumsily at the head of the group, sporadically looking back over his fuzzy rump to make sure they all followed but saying nothing whatsoever.

Nolan and Winnie, however, filled what would have been the determined silence with friendly—if somewhat breathless—chatter. Nolan seemed to have a boundless curiosity about the Depths now that he was seeing it with his own eyes, and Winnie provided answers where she could. Early in their ascent, she tossed some questions over to Tod, but once it became clear Tod wasn't going to answer, she made a game of pestering him with questions, Nolan grinning silently beside her all the while.

Finally, after much puffing, scrambling, and slipping, they crested the rise and emerged onto a flat, grassy plain. A sea of springy, green grass spread out before them, higher than Winnie's head, bobbing in a warm breeze that produced a constant, pleasant susurration.

Nolan looked around with his mouth hanging open.

"Of course," he said at last. "Of course we climbed out of a crater in a mountain and ended up on a plain. Tod, how—"

"Would you just shut up?" Tod spat, turning to face Nolan. "Between you and this one"—he jerked a thumb in Winnie's direction—"it's impossible to think! All I hear is *yak yak yak!*"

At the sound of Tod's raised voice, Gerald, who had begun following a well-trampled path through the high grass, popped his head up over the undulating crop and bleated, "Llama! I. Am. A. Llama!"

His head disappeared from view again as he carried on up the path.

Winnie, stone-faced, watched as color rose in Tod's pallid cheeks. Without comment, he took off after the ungulate, spitefully kicking a dirt clod out of his way as he went.

When he'd disappeared down the path, Winnie turned to Nolan, biting her lip to contain the burble of laughter that threatened to burst out of her. Nolan's face was crimson with the same effort. She wound her arm around his, reveling in the secret mirth they shared at Tod's expense, and pulled him forward onto the hard dirt trail.

"Explain to me why there's a talking llama here," Nolan said when they'd gotten close enough to the others to keep them in sight but not so close that their conversation would be overheard.

"Nina told me once that sometimes essences take the form of animals. It's not very common, I think, but it does happen."

"You're telling me this guy was a person before he died and then showed up here as a big, weird horse with three stomachs?"

"Yes? Mostly? Are llamas related to horses? Don't they have four stomachs?"

"You're thinking of cows," Nolan answered. "And actually, I don't think they're related to horses, but they kind of look like they should be."

"I was thinking he looks a bit like a kangaroo. Just in the face, I mean…"

"Here's what I don't understand," Nolan interrupted, trying to get their conversation back on track. "Why would a person want to spend eternity as a llama?"

Winnie shrugged. "I really couldn't say. It wouldn't be my first choice, but I suppose there are worse things to be. You could ask Gerald."

Nolan's brow furrowed. "I don't feel like he'd be open to interrogation."

"Maybe not," Winnie conceded.

She watched the siblings moving up ahead of them. The grass through which they walked had begun to thin, and they strode side-by-side now, Winnie's arm occasionally brushing against Nolan's in a way she found quite pleasant.

Nolan had fallen quiet, and Winnie glanced over at his profile. She followed his gaze; it was focused on the back of Tod's head.

"I'm sorry he snapped at you. He's just anxious about finding his daughter," she said.

Nolan glowered. "Why are you apologizing for that creep?"

Winnie blinked. "Well...he's my brother-in-law."

"So that makes him trustworthy?" Nolan prodded. "Look, Winnie, I know you're in a weird position because of your sister and the baby, but I trust Tod about as much as I trust anything else in this place."

"Nolan, do you really think he had something to do with this?"

"Why not? You're talking about a guy who met his wife by kidnapping her and keeping her locked in a cage. That's not a dating strategy, Winnie. That's a felony."

Winnie bit her lip. She'd shared these same concerns from the beginning, but the reality of the situation— Verna's apparent desire to be with Tod and the arrival of baby Ren—had made it easier to push those concerns to the back of her mind. Clearly Nolan had done no such thing.

"I know the situation is less than ideal..."

Nolan snorted at this understatement. "Less than ideal would be if one of them had an inconvenient commute or if they couldn't agree on whether or not to raise their kid vegan. We're talking about basing a whole relationship on lies, cruelty, and brainwashing."

"You don't think we can trust him? At all?"

"No. Not one bit. We have a united purpose at the moment, so we have to make do. But once this is over, I'm sure Nina will be in no mood to stay here, and that...*monster* is going to have to find himself a new lackey. I suggest you do what you can to convince your sister to get out from under his thumb as well."

Winnie cringed at the thought of that conversation. Trying to tell Verna anything she didn't want to hear was unpleasant, but convincing her she should leave her husband, Ren's father? She shuddered.

"I don't know. People do change, don't they? And I can't see him putting his daughter in harm's way." She looked at Vita, who had moved closer to her brother to talk quietly. "What if Vita's the one we can't trust?"

"What makes her a more likely suspect than him?" Nolan asked.

"Nothing, I suppose. It's just weird, isn't it? That she showed up out of the blue on the night Ren disappeared? I mean, Tod had never even mentioned her before. Verna said he was always sort of cagey about his family. And now here she is, leading us..."

"They're *both* leading us," Nolan reminded her. "I have no idea if she's trustworthy, but I won't be surprised to find out they're working together."

"Working together to achieve what?" Winnie asked, finally voicing a niggling concern that she'd turned over many times in her mind in the last several hours. "What's the point of kidnapping a sweet baby?"

Nolan was silent for a time, and when he spoke, his voice was almost a whisper.

"Winnie, if you and your sisters have power over the seasons, and Tod has power over the dead, and Vita has power over health...what power will Renata have?"

Winnie looked up to meet his gaze. "I don't know, Nolan. I just...I don't know."

They walked in silence for a while after that, lost in their own worries. From time to time, one of them commented on some point of the landscape.

Nolan pointed up in awe once when a flock of leathery, prehistoric reptiles glided by above them. His mouth hanging open, he sputtered "ptero...ptero..." several times before Winnie said "yes, birdasauruses" in a soothing tone and dragged him along by one hand to catch up with the others.

Sometime later, they crossed a bridge, and all four bipeds paused for a moment to watch a tentacled monster pass lazily beneath them, its thousands of suckers glistening wetly when one great arm, broader than a train car and longer than the whole train it would couple to, raised out of the water to gain purchase on the side of the bridge.

But what shook Winnie the most was passing an anchor pool, a larger version of the small pools Winnie made every week to chat with Nina. A shallow, stone structure, it passed in and out of sight between the strangers milling around it. The essences at the pool paid no attention to the passersby, but Nolan watched them solemnly, studying the faces of those who stood or knelt at its lip, gazing into it as if into a deep well rather than into a few inches of water. Of course, Winnie knew it wasn't the water they saw but their anchors, the people they loved in life and who themselves would one day pass over and release the pool-gazers. The vision in the pool was deeply personal; the first time she'd witnessed pool-gazing, she hadn't needed Abel, whose job it was to connect those who had recently died with the essences that had been anchored to them here in the Depths, to tell her not to look into a pool. Though it was peaceful and quite poignant to watch, the taboo nature of peeping at someone else's anchor had been almost tangible.

When the anchor pool passed out of sight, and Nolan's attention turned back to the road ahead, Winnie caught his eye. She smiled reassuringly, and he smiled back, but there was something sad in it, and Winnie let the knowledge that death awaited Nolan, as it did his sister, wash painfully over her. She, her parents, her sisters, and all other beings like them wouldn't share that fate. She could be destroyed, her body obliterated and her consciousness diffused into nothingness so that it might coalesce again in a new form, but she wouldn't age and wilt the way these mortals she had grown so fond of would someday. It was one of the few details about Other magic her parents had made sure she and her sisters understood. She looked away from Nolan, losing herself in swirling thoughts she rarely indulged.

Winnie scarcely noticed as the hard-packed dirt beneath their feet gave way to gravel and then to cobblestone; when she finally registered their surroundings, she discovered they were on a narrow road flanked by shadowy, old-growth forest.

They'd certainly covered a lot of ground in...how long *had* they been walking? She asked Nolan.

"Not for too long, I think. Er...actually, I guess it has been a while. Come to think of it, we've been walking forever!" He seemed upset by this realization, looking around as if he might see a complaint desk nearby where he could vent his spleen.

"Never mind, Nolan," Winnie said soothingly. "It doesn't matter. It's this place. It messes everything up."

Unconvinced, Nolan pulled out his phone, but Winnie could tell from his furrowed brow that it was no help.

"Did your battery die?" she asked.

"No, it's fine, but I can't…What time did we come through the door?"

Winnie pondered. "I don't know," she shrugged.

"I don't either. I'm looking at these numbers, but…Winnie, it's like they don't make any sense to me."

"Forget it," Vita said, coming alongside them. "You won't be able to figure that stuff out here. Time, distance, direction…they aren't the same here. Things will go back to normal if we get back to the living world."

Winnie's head shot up. "*If?* Don't you mean *when*, Vita?"

Vita returned Winnie's gaze. "Sure. Of course I do." She moved away again, closing the distance to her brother with her long strides.

Nolan's arm brushed Winnie's again, and she glanced at him. "Maybe you're right not to trust her," he intoned darkly.

Sometime later—clearly, Winnie couldn't have said how long—Gerald's clopping gait slowed, and he turned to allow the bipeds straggling behind him to catch up.

"Here we are," he said when they'd all gathered in a loose circle. He stood in front of a colossal boulder that jutted up through the forest floor, its weather-beaten face etched with wear and streaked with the dirt of untold years.

Winnie sighed, thinking of her father. "Dad would dig this," she said wistfully to no one in particular.

Gerald emitted what might have been interpreted by a generous listener in a noisy room as a chuckle.

"Oh, no, no…there's no digging required, madam! We just have to go through the door."

Winnie held up a finger to clarify, but Nolan reached out and gently pushed her hand down, shaking his head with a sympathetic *let it go* look. Winnie sighed.

Gerald turned and headed into the forest surrounding the boulder, circling around behind the great rock. Tod followed unquestioningly, and the others fell in behind him. They tramped over leaf fall and sparse groundcover; unlike the prairie path they'd followed at the lip of the caldera, there was little evidence here of frequent traffic. Wherever Gerald was leading them, it was off the beaten path.

When they reached the far side of the rock, at a place where the encroaching trees threatened to make further progress impossible, Gerald pulled up short. The gaggle of two-legged followers crowded around him, and Winnie, disadvantaged by her height, wormed between Vita and Tod to get a look at what they'd stopped for. To her surprise, she saw that he stood before a grimy, ill-defined door cleverly tucked beneath a jutting, rocky overhang. She shivered, thinking about the last time she'd passed through a door in the Depths.

Tod stepped forward as if to put a hand on the door, but Vita stopped him. "Are you sure that's a good idea?"

Tod turned to look at her questioningly.

"No one knows we're here, remember? It's a good bet the old man is in there somewhere; you'll give yourself away the moment you use your power to open that door."

"Of course," Tod answered, shaking himself to restore reason. "Of course. I wasn't thinking."

Winnie caught a look on Vita's face that made her unsure. Concern, maybe? Even…skepticism? But as quickly as the expression surfaced, it disappeared, and at that moment Winnie was distracted by Gerald shouldering his way between Vita and Tod to approach the door.

"No need for you to open it," he barked in his bleating voice. "I wedged it open on my way out."

Sure enough, with a gentle nudge from his banana-shaped muzzle, the door swung inward, revealing a stone passage shrouded in darkness. He marched through first, his leathery pads making muted *thuk thuk* sounds on the stone. Tod followed, and Vita trailed him, leaving only Winnie and Nolan behind.

Winnie looked at Nolan, whose Adam's apple bobbed comically as he surveyed the darkness beyond the door. She could hardly blame him for feeling trepidation after what happened the last time they passed through a door together.

"Well," he said finally, taking a bracing breath. "Ladies first."

He held out a welcoming arm, and her sympathy of moments earlier evaporated. Pulling off her sunglasses and stuffing them in her backpack, she rolled her eyes as she led him into the dark unknown.

Twenty

Winnie's sense of déjà vu heightened as they began making their way down a stone corridor, following the sure guidance of the llama in the lead. Like last time, when she'd had Abel and Nina by her side, torchieres lined the walls of the dark passage, casting flickering, insubstantial light on the path they followed.

What had waited for her at the end of that corridor was both the thing they sought and the thing that made her life immeasurably more difficult. Finding Verna had been a gratifying relief: the return of her sister hadn't just put the family back into balance but the seasons as well. The look on her father's face when they'd emerged from the tunnels beneath his rock shop had been worth the terrible strain and fear the journey had engendered in her, and though her mother had, as ever, maintained a brave façade throughout Verna's disappearance, even she had cried joyfully when she once again wrapped her daughter in her arms.

But Tod had been an unexpected and unwelcome addition to the family. After the initial rows following their daughter's return, Pete and Brooke had voiced their continued concerns subtly but persistently. Verna had listened, but it was clear to her sisters that she was humoring their parents rather than seriously considering their apprehension about the circumstances under which their daughter had met her mate and the repercussions of that meeting on her emotional wellbeing.

Finally, Verna had assured them she was well and truly in love: she had never been mistreated by her captor, she had willingly engaged him in conversation when the opportunity permitted, and he had never been anything but kind to her in the weeks and months that followed.

And then Renata had come along, and all their concerns about Tod and Verna were subsumed by their immediate and immeasurable love for the soft-skinned bundle that relationship had produced. The family's early concerns seemed so much less immediate when there was Ren to focus on: Ren's first coos and giggles, Ren's smiles and gurgles, Ren's first tooth poking through her bottom gum. By the time she took her first steps and began happy, disjointed babbling, concern for her parents' situation had been pushed with little regret or resistance to the back of the collective Harvester mind. It was just easier that way.

"What are you thinking about?" Nolan asked quietly from behind her.

Winnie snapped her attention back to the present.

"Just thinking about the last time I was here," she answered.

"Here in this corridor?" Nolan asked. He jogged a little to fall in beside her.

"No. Well...I don't know. This place is so complicated. I guess it might have been the same one. It looks the same. But we definitely didn't come through the same door."

"You came through the zombie door, right? That's what Nina told me."

Winnie snorted. "I'd forgotten she called them that. They weren't really zombies, you know. Just tortured essences."

"A torture they deserved, from what my sister said." Nolan's voice was uncharacteristically cold.

"Yes, I've thought a lot about that, and I agree with you. Regardless, that was the door we came through, but there's no reason to think both doors couldn't lead to the exact same place. That would sort of figure here."

Nolan chuckled. "From the stories Nina's told me, there's not much that couldn't happen here." He was silent for a few moments, considering his own words. "To be honest, I don't think I totally believed that until today. I'm not saying I didn't believe what she was telling me," he added hastily in response to her quirked brow. "I just mean that I couldn't quite wrap my head around it: who you are and what this place really is and what her job is here...it just seemed too unreal to be real. Now, of course, after the birdbath and the..." He trailed off, and Winnie glanced over at him.

"The Nights?" she supplied, and he observed her warily as if afraid she might resent him bringing them up.

"Yeah. Those. Now that I've seen that stuff..."

His thought went unfinished as up ahead Gerald's clopping stopped, and he turned to face them.

"This is where I must leave you," he informed them.

"Fine," Vita responded, crossing her strong arms over her chest and squaring her feet in a gesture that made Winnie glad she was on their side.

Probably, the niggling voice of doubt whispered in her mind. She forced it down. Now wasn't the time to reexamine Vita's trustworthiness.

"You know where you're going, of course." This was a statement, not a question, and Gerald directed it at Tod, who glanced briefly at Winnie before grunting his assent. "Good," Gerald finished. "Then I wish you four all the best."

He cut between them unceremoniously and began walking back the way they'd come.

Feeling that someone should say something, Winnie called after him, "Thanks for the help, Gerald!"

He paused and turned to look at her, his long lashes quivering as he regarded her.

"Don't thank me yet, Elemental. Coming here and finding Abel is only the first step. I've seen what you're up against."

Beside her, Winnie heard Nolan swallow loudly.

"But," Gerald continued with dignity, "I meant it when I wished you the best. I've been here a long time, perhaps longer than even I understand. And what's happened here isn't the way of things. The Depths and the Above are separated by what lies between the doors for a reason: they aren't meant to blend. What happens above and what happens here ought to stay separated." He looked pointedly at Tod. "Those beings who belong above have no place here, and those whose place is here should not wander around above."

Tod sneered. "Thanks for your thoughts on the way of things, fur ball, but I think we can handle it from here."

Gerald gazed at Tod steadily with camelid disdain—Winnie marveled that there even was such a thing—and then turned and clopped away unhurriedly, his stubby tail flicking desultorily as he melted into the shadows.

"Ass," Tod muttered, as the group of four turned and continued walking, and from behind them, an echoing voice asserted one last time, *"Llama!"*

Twenty-One

As the foursome continued down the corridor, Vita and Tod walking side-by-side in the lead and Nolan trudging along beside Winnie in the rear, Winnie began to feel, once again, that more time had gone by than seemed possible. Nothing changed around them: the view ahead and behind them, step after step, was identical. The same torchieres spaced evenly, the same dancing shadows, the same dark terminus cutting off the view in both directions.

She was just opening her mouth to ask Tod if he actually knew where they were going, when he suddenly tensed, paused, and raised a warning hand. Turning his head slightly, he motioned for them to be quiet. Winnie felt the skin on her arms prickle, and when she looked at Nolan, he was wide-eyed, his glasses sliding down his nose unnoticed as he peered at the darkness ahead of Tod.

Moving silent as a shadow, Tod stepped back against a span of bare wall between two torchieres. He motioned for the others to follow.

When they were tucked against the stone together, he whispered in a low voice, "We're at the hub. We need to decide on a strategy now before we get any closer."

"What's the hub?" Nolan asked, and Vita answered him without taking her eyes off of her brother.

"It's like command central for the afterlife."

"So, this is where my sister should be? I mean, this is where she is when she contacts me?"

Something chirped in Winnie's mind at his question, but she couldn't quite put a finger on what it was.

"Yes," Tod answered. "We need to go in quietly and see what's happening in there. If the old man is there, this could be our chance to confront him and figure out why he's here."

"What?" Nolan said loudly, and Tod shushed him with an aggressive *shhh!*

"Don't *shhh* me, Tod. We didn't come down here to work out your family drama, remember? We came here for two people and two only: your daughter and my sister. We're not going anywhere near your father. If you two have a bone to pick with dear old dad, you'll have to save it for Thanksgiving dinner like the rest of us do!"

Tod's face flushed angrily as he listened to this dressing down, but to Winnie's surprise, it was Vita who spoke next.

"I agree with Nolan. We need to make sure the little girl and...?"

"Nina!" Winnie and Nolan supplied in unison. Winnie screwed up her face in disapproval.

"Right, yes, Nina. We need to make sure the girl and Nina are secure before we deal with the old man or whoever else might be responsible for all this."

Tod studied her darkly, but finally he looked at Winnie, who nodded her vigorous approval. Clearly, he was outnumbered.

"Fine," he agreed at last. "We'll find them first."

Winnie tensed with the expectation of movement, but Tod simply stood before her, looking back and forth among them.

"Right," Winnie volunteered once the pause became awkward. "So, why don't we go do that? Now."

"I'd love to," Tod answered. "But I don't know where they are. Part of the reason I wanted to confront whoever did this was to find out from him where my daughter is."

"Who sent Gerald?" Vita chimed in.

The other three looked at her.

"Oh!" Winnie exclaimed. "Of course! Abel! Abel sent Gerald." She looked around as if Abel might suddenly pop out from behind one of the torchiere poles. He didn't. "If Abel sent Gerald, why wasn't he waiting for us when Gerald left? He should be here to meet us." She frowned, and a new worm of worry burrowed into her gut.

"Abel is resourceful. I'm sure he's fine," Tod opined.

"If he were fine, he'd be here. He adores Nina."

Tod raised a skeptical eyebrow.

"Doubt that all you want, but I know he does," she insisted. "He just has a...curmudgeonly way of showing it."

Tod snorted, and Winnie waved him away.

"Say what you will, but if Nina's in trouble, I know for a fact he'd do whatever he could to help her." Winnie felt duty-bound to defend Abel.

Nolan cleared his throat. "I hate to point this out, but isn't this the same guy who led you down into the most dangerous part of the Depths on his boss's orders for his own gain?"

"Well, it sounds bad when you put it that way...," Winnie trailed off.

The four of them fell back into silence.

"How do we find them?" Nolan asked finally, and Winnie looked up sharply at the despondency in his voice.

"We'll find them, Nolan!" she insisted, reaching out for his hand. Squeezing it, she insisted again, "I promise you we'll find them. If Nina and I made it this far, I'm sure...," her voice trailed off, and her uncanny, white eyes glossed over as a series of thoughts clicked into place in her mind.

Startling Nolan, she snapped fingers. "Tod! Where was Verna?"

Tod stared at her blankly. "What do you mean?"

"When you brought Verna here, you must have kept her somewhere she couldn't leave."

"Well, yes, that's true," Tod answered, shifting his weight and sniffing.

"Okay...so where was it?"

Vita cut in. "You're thinking that wherever your sister was kept might be where we'll find Nina or Renata?"

"Yep," Winnie responded, never taking her eyes off her brother-in-law who, rather suspiciously, didn't seem as enthusiastic about her theory as Vita.

"I don't think that's likely." Tod's gaze now focused on his feet, which were busily kicking pebbles back and forth.

"Why?" his three companions asked in unison, and Winnie felt the atmosphere shift from optimism that this might be a lead worth following to misgiving over Tod's hesitancy.

Nolan made a noise like a man opening a jug of milk to find it curdled and lumpy.

"Let me guess," he said, his voice dripping with undisguised disgust. "You don't want your sister and sister-in-law to see where you kept your wife before you decided to marry her rather than kill her to get your way."

Even though the dim, flickering light of the torches made it hard to discern expressions, Winnie was sure she saw Tod's eyes darken.

"You don't know what the hell you're talking about."

Nolan pushed his glasses up his nose and puffed out his chest bravely. "Then prove me wrong."

Winnie looked back from Nolan to Tod, and across from her, she saw Vita do the same thing.

Tod glared at Nolan in the half-light.

"I have apologized for the circumstances that led to my marriage. You seem to be intent on continuing to punish me. It would be nice if you could be as gracious in receiving an apology as I was in offering one."

Winnie raised a finger to respond to this, but Vita beat her to it.

"We don't have time for this. We know Winnie and Nolan's vote, and here's mine: take us to wherever you kept Verna."

Winnie gazed at Vita, girl-crushing begrudgingly at this display of brook-no-argument badassery. She still suspected the worst of Vita, but a growing part of her hoped fervently that those suspicions were wrong.

If Tod considered talking back to his sister, he thought better of it.

"Fine. Wrong, but fine. Keep up and keep quiet." With that, he swung around and headed back down the corridor they'd been following, his long, rapid strides once again forcing the two slighter members of the rescue party to jog to keep up.

"Say what you will about Tod," she muttered to Nolan, "but I haven't gotten this much cardio in weeks."

Perhaps because she'd been distracted by her conversation with Nolan as they'd walked this corridor in the opposite direction, Winnie was surprised when they stopped before a door, nestled in the shadows between two torchieres. From the look on Nolan's face, he shared her surprise.

"Was this here the first time we came this way?" he asked her in a whisper, and she shrugged unhelpfully.

"In this place, who knows?" she responded. Tod pulled the door open, and Winnie peered into the gloom beyond the entryway: it looked like another tunnel, but there was no way to see where it headed.

The tunnel itself was much smaller than the one they'd been navigating, and its narrow dimensions meant they'd have to walk single-file in what looked like total darkness.

"Why, though?" Nolan whinged, though so quietly only Winnie could hear. "Why does every place we need to get to have to be at the end of a terrifyingly dark tunnel?"

Winnie reached for his wrist with one hand and snagged the back of Vita's blouse with the other just before the latter disappeared into the darkness.

"It's the afterlife, Nolan. What did you think there'd be, fairy lights?"

He grumbled a response, but Winnie was too focused on keeping up with Vita and not losing hold of Nolan to pay him any more attention. She shambled along in the cloaking darkness, her senses once again alert as they had been during their flight from the Nights. The mere thought of them made her stomach turn over, and as she shuffled along, she told herself over and over that they would not be here. Just because this passage was dark, it didn't mean there was anything lurking in that darkness.

Her mind said these words, but her stomach refused to listen. Desperate to calm herself, she closed her eyes tightly and tried to breathe deeply and evenly, willing herself to calm down.

Wham! Something hard and immovable stopped her short. Winnie gasped, and her eyes flew open, terror at the thought of what she'd see flooding her limbs with molten heat.

But all she saw before her was bare stone.

"Girl," Vita said, studying Winnie from a foot to the right, where she'd stopped after navigating the bend that Winnie hadn't seen coming. Tod had already rounded the next corner and was out of sight. "What are you doing? Walking with your eyes closed?" Vita's tone was prodding but good-humored, and Winnie could see that she was grinning.

"Oh! I can see you!" she exclaimed when Vita's expression finally registered.

"It's been getting lighter," Nolan put in, stepping out of the narrow passage behind her. "Winnie, can you see me?" His tone was concerned. He turned to Vita and asked, "Do you think this is an effect of the…you know…eye thing?" He mumbled this last bit with his lips pressed mostly closed, his mouth screwed around comically to point in Vita's direction.

"Nolan, I can see. And even if I couldn't, I'd still be able to hear you."

"Oh," he said, pushing up his glasses once again. "Then why did you walk into the—"

"Let's see what's around the next corner, huh?" Winnie said with gusto, squeezing her way past Vita and avoiding eye contact with Nolan. "We don't want to lose Tod if—"

"Winnie?" a voice from the shadowy darkness beyond the winding turns called out.

Before Winnie could respond, Nolan was pushing past her and calling out to the voice, "Nina? Is that you?"

Twenty-Two

Winnie burst to life at the sound of Nina's voice and took off after Nolan, following him so closely through the tortuous passage that she stepped on his heels several times. Ahead of Nolan, she saw Tod's wiry form rounding another corner. Clearly, this corridor had been designed to slow any trespassers and obscure their view of the path ahead.

Nolan called out to his sister as they rounded the final bend, and, moving faster than Winnie, he dodged to one side to avoid colliding with Tod, who had stopped before the barred door separating the newcomers from the prisoners within. Winnie, disadvantaged by Nolan's back blocking her view, managed to plow into Tod, scrabbling to stay upright and frantically searching the space they'd entered simultaneously.

If Tod gave her a dirty look, she didn't notice. She was too focused on the round, blue eyes that gazed into hers. Ren's eyes.

"Ren!" she wailed, climbing over Tod's still-off-balance body to thrust an arm through the bars toward her niece. "Ren! Baby! I'm so happy to see you!"

Ren was sitting upright on a small bed, her fine hair mashed against one side of her head. The three of them entering had clearly woken the little girl. Winnie gazed at her, her joy souring just slightly at the look on Ren's face. Something in her look seemed…fearful?

Before Winnie could ponder this, Nina's voice cut across her thoughts.

"Winnie! I…"

Nina pulled away from Nolan, who stood like Winnie with his arms thrust through the cell bars to hug his sister. Nina reached out for Winnie's hands, but she stood holding them in hers, gazing at Winnie.

"Oh, Nina, I'm so relieved! I was so afraid…," Winnie trailed off, studying her friend's face. "Nina? Are you okay?"

"Winnie…what happened to your eyes?"

Winnie almost melted with relief. "Oh jeez, of course!" She turned to look at Ren again, who was still studying her somberly.

"Ren, it's just me, baby. It's just plain, old Auntie Woo."

Ren turned her head ever so slightly, as if the change in Winnie's eye color might simply be a trick of the light.

A sudden thought occurred to Winnie, and she dug the sunglasses Nolan had given her out of her backpack. Slipping them on, she smiled at her niece.

"Annie Woo?" Ren asked, her tiny voice both breaking and mending Winnie's heart. She hadn't realized just how frightened she'd been. Perhaps she simply hadn't allowed herself to acknowledge how much fear the loss of this little person could engender in her.

"Hi, sweet girl," Winnie said, whispering to hide how heavy and unmanageable her own voice seemed in that moment.

Nina released her hands, and Winnie squatted, holding the bars that separated her from her niece as

Ren slid off her bed carefully and waddled over to her aunt. Winnie pulled her carefully against the bars, pressing her own face as far between them as possible to kiss the girl's cheeks and forehead and even nose.

Over her shoulder, she heard Tod clear his throat, and she turned to look back up at him.

He stood over them, gazing down at his daughter.

"Hi, Daddy," Ren gabbled, looking up into his face as if he'd just come from the supermarket rather than from another plane of existence.

"Hello, Ren. Winnie?" He made a sweeping gesture to the side, which Winnie had to admit was slightly nicer than he might have done, considering she had practically knocked him down and stomped over him to get to his daughter first.

She straightened and scooted out of his way, turning her attention once again to Nina, whose red-rimmed eyes shone with recent tears.

Winnie reached through the bars for Nina's hands and said, "I'm so glad to see you."

Nina grinned. "Me too. Falsies."

Winnie's mouth dropped open. "Huh?"

"Falsies. That's what you need to complete this…," she trailed off but circled the air in front of Winnie with spayed fingers to explain what needed completion.

Winnie looked down at her decolletage dubiously. "I don't know, Nina. I have a hard enough time finding blouses that look good on the girls."

"Umm…," a voice to Winnie's left said, and she looked up in surprise to see Nolan looking at a space over her head, unblinking.

"Uhh…," she said to his Adam's apple.

"So…," he responded.

Winnie's brain clicked back into inconvenient action. "Introduce Vita!" she half-shouted awkwardly, and Nolan snapped in response and turned to fetch her.

Winnie turned a wilting expression on Nina, who pushed her glasses up her nose and said seriously, "How can you stand that chemistry?"

Winnie groaned. "Well, at least he didn't overhear me awkwardly talking about my boobs." She rolled her eyes.

Nina's brow creased. "Your boobs? Oh! Ha! I meant false *eyelashes*, Winnie! For your new eyes!" Nina looked critically at Winnie's chest. "Yes. No. I definitely don't think you should change those."

Despite her lingering embarrassment, Winnie grinned at her friend.

"I'm so glad to see you, Nina," she said again, and the two friends hugged through the bars that separated them.

"This is sweet, but we need to get out of here," Vita said by way of introduction.

Winnie pulled away from Nina and turned to face Vita.

"I'm sure Nina is happy to meet you, too," she said sardonically, but neither Vita nor Nina seemed phased by her tone.

"Hi!" Nina said, thrusting a hand through the bars at Vita. "I'm Nina. Did you move into 3A? Did they find out where that smell was coming from?"

Winnie marveled that Vita, for the time since they'd met, looked a little off-balance.

"The smell...?" she repeated uncertainly, and Winnie began to giggle.

"Nina, she's not our neighbor. I promise you're the only other person from our building that I'd ever recruit to bring to the afterlife."

"Oh!" Nina smiled. "Of course. Duh." She rolled her eyes good-humoredly. "So how did you two meet?" Nina rested her weight on one foot, one hand on her hip and the other under her chin, studying Vita like a cocktail party hostess cordially greeting a late arrival instead of a detainee in an underground, metal cage.

Vita turned to Winnie. "This explains so much about Nolan," she said. Winnie just shrugged in response.

Vita turned to respond to Nina, but the sound of her brother's raised voice drew her attention.

"I'm telling you I don't have one," he said forcefully to Nolan, and Nolan, despite the significant height differential, drew himself up like a size-blind terrier.

"Well, you're the only one here with experience keeping people in cages, so I suggest you find one," he shouted up at Tod.

Vita crossed the space to them in two long strides. "What's the problem?" she asked, and beside her, Winnie heard Nina breathe a little *ooh* of admiration.

"I know, right? She has one setting, and that setting is *just try it, bub,*" Winnie whispered. Nina nodded appreciatively, and the two friends turned back to the unfolding drama.

"The problem is that your brother doesn't have a key to his own cage!"

"Brother?" Nina whispered, and Winnie nodded vigorously, glancing down at the top of Ren's head as Nina bent to scoop her up and settle her on her hip, a move so practiced and fluid that Winnie could tell she'd done it many times. She silently thanked the powers that be for giving Ren a good caretaker during her ordeal.

"My cage? *My* cage?" Tod demanded. "You're accusing me of building this...*thing*?" Tod motioned at the cage with a sweep of his hand.

Nolan, now bouncing up onto his tiptoes, nodded his affirmation aggressively, which made his glasses slip.

"That's preposterous! How dare you," Tod hissed.

Nolan made a noise of protest, but Vita raised her hands to signal calm.

Tod went on as if she weren't there. "If you've got something to say to me, tiny, go ahead and say it," Tod spat.

"*Tiny?*" Nolan asked incredulously. "Oh, that's rich! That's the first time I've been name-called by a guy who looks like...like...like a Dracula doll someone left in the back window of their car for too long!"

Winnie looked at Nina with one eyebrow cocked, and Nina shrugged the shoulder not weighed down by Renata.

"He's never been very good at trash-talking," she said.

179

Nolan's wobbly jab gave Vita the opening she needed.

"Both of you need to shut up now," she barked at the men, and Tod, waving a hand in disgust, turned away from his diminutive opponent.

Undeterred, Vita continued talking. "I think we've established that Tod doesn't have a key for the cell. Is that right?" she asked her brother's turned back. He grunted.

"Even though he should," Nolan cut in, "since this is *his* cell that he kept his *wife* in."

From the corner of her eye, Winnie saw Nina rush to press Ren's head against her shoulder with the palm of her hand, effectively covering both of Ren's ears. Nolan must have caught the movement too because he had the good sense to look a little shamefaced at airing dirty laundry in front of Renata.

"So, we need to find another way of getting these two out of this cell," Vita finished with a stern glance in Nolan's direction.

"Perhaps I can help with that," said a gravelly voice, and Winnie spun to face the menacing stranger who had just emerged from the passageway behind them.

Twenty-Three

A man stood there, as tall as Tod or Vita but substantially broader, with matted, unkempt hair that fell past his shoulders. His great, lumpen form was wrapped in a coarse cloth robe tied around his middle. Dark stains and stiff, crusty patches speckled its expanse, and Winnie's nose crinkled as the smell of its filth reached her: pungently ripe body smells mingled with the prickling odor of garbage.

Underneath it all, another smell turned her stomach: the smell of decay, of old meat left to bloat in the heat.

Buzzing reached Winnie's ears, and she grimaced when she realized the sound came from darting flies that circled the man's head and shoulders. Gazing at the man's face through the slight distortion of Nolan's sunglasses, Winnie felt her gorge rise.

The flies weren't circling the man's face. They were living in it.

Suppurative sores dotted the man's cheeks and brow, which were misshapen by scars; a particularly nasty one ran from the corner of one eye to his lip. A ghastly, purple-red boil on the side of his nose oozed steadily. Winnie watched in horrified thrall as a single maggot squirmed in a moist glob that trailed from the ulcerated carbuncle and fell unceremoniously onto the man's filthy tunic.

Behind her, she heard Nina murmuring to Renata; she'd clearly turned away from this interloper and was distracting Ren. Winnie's heart swelled with gratitude, even as it beat double-time with fear.

She felt a brush against her arm, and Vita's warm hand slipped into hers, a warm rush of calming energy spreading up Winnie's arm and into her chest.

"Winnie," Vita said quietly beside her. "Meet Damion Strife."

Winnie didn't speak. She was determined not to look away from the black, soulless gaze of the man who she now knew for certain had stolen her niece from under her sleeping nose and imprisoned her best friend. She doubted he could even see that her eyes stayed locked on his from behind the sunglasses she still wore, but she didn't care. *She* knew she was staring him down, and that was enough.

"So, you're the pesky little Elemental I've heard so much about."

"That's me," she responded, and she was surprised that her voice came out clear and strong. Feeling emboldened, she added, "If you think I was a pest before, wait until I walk out of here with these two." She gestured back over her shoulder at Nina and Ren.

Strife studied her, his hulking form eerily still even as the insect contingent that traveled with him buzzed, swarmed, and wriggled around his weeping pustules. Winnie tried her best to focus on his eyes and nothing else for the sake of her roiling gut. Something told her that throwing up on Strife's shoes would significantly diminish the Vita-esque gravitas she was trying to project.

Without warning, Strife emitted a damp, garbled sound, something between a cough and a retch. Winnie leaned back slightly, unsure what the noise presaged but certain that, given the disgusting state of his outsides, anything he might be preparing to expel from his insides would be downright hazardous.

Strife made the sound again several times in a row, and Winnie realized with growing distress that his pestilential body was producing *laughter*. It was the first time that hearing someone laugh made her want to take a long, hot shower.

Vita approached her father, stepping between him and Winnie and raising her voice to be heard over the big man's soggy expulsions.

"Enough, old man. Whatever you thought you were going to accomplish with this little stunt is done. We're here for the woman and the girl. Open the door."

Strife continued to hack disgustingly, but his black gaze shifted to Vita's face. Despite his apparent mirth at their rescue attempt, his eyes remained cold and assessing, and Winnie knew for certain that despite his disheveled appearance, his mind was orderly and well-controlled. She shivered.

"Why would I want to open the door?" Strife asked his daughter, the last of his laughter finally abating with a wheeze.

"Because whatever your plan was, I'm going to make sure it doesn't happen."

Strife snorted. "And how do you plan to do that?" he asked. "You're way out of your element down here, and I'm very much in mine." As he said this, he wormed a hand down into the folds of his robe and withdrew it again, his large fist closed tightly so that all Winnie could see were the grimy creases of his knuckles and the blackened, rough-edged thumbnail.

He turned his hand palm up and opened it; Winnie and Vita recoiled in unison. A bloated mouse corpse lay in his palm, juices dribbling from its split belly between Strife's fingers.

Within seconds, the swarming flies had picked up the scent of the mouse and began crawling over the tiny form. Strife looked down, and Winnie was appalled at the expression that crossed his face. To her, it hinted at affection, paternal affection even, eerily similar and yet worlds away from the look of serene pride her own father had worn the day of Ren's birth when his daughters and granddaughter had surrounded him.

Winnie couldn't help herself: she looked away, repulsed.

So it came as a great surprise to her when Vita grabbed her forearm and yanked her aside so that the large man didn't land on her when he suddenly, silently collapsed.

Twenty-Four

"...the hell?" Winnie muttered under her breath as she looked down at the fallen man at her feet. She lifted one foot to nudge him with her toe when Nina's voice distracted her.

"Abel!"

Winnie's head shot up, and she followed Nina's gaze, a smile splitting her face when she saw Abel standing at the entrance to the passage, the doused, iron head of a torchiere in his hand. He looked exactly as he had the first time they'd met when she and Nina had passed through the liminal space between worlds and come through a door on a lone hilltop. He'd appeared that day as part of his duties as a steward wraith, untethered beings whose living anchors had forgotten or forsaken them, and who were thus indentured to the afterlife for an undetermined term of service in the hopes of someday earning the right to pass on. His wiry hair still frizzed out from his scalp in a black halo, and his dour, heavy-lidded eyes scanned the room uninterestedly, as if knocking out a dangerous usurper to assist a motley rescue brigade was a perfectly typical afternoon activity.

"Abel, you badass!" Winnie crowed, reaching over Strife's prone form to punch Abel on the arm.

He cringed away from her, looking at the spot she'd punched as if he might see a dent there.

"You seem happy I knocked out Strife, so why are you assaulting me?"

Winnie grinned sheepishly at having forgotten that Abel's tolerance for shenanigans hadn't increased over the many years he'd been dead.

"Sorry. It was a congratulatory punch."

Abel didn't return her grin. "Well, it hurt."

Nolan piped up to agree. "She hit me once like that, too. It does hurt."

Winnie scowled at him, and he chuckled, pushing his glasses up his nose as he held her gaze.

"Oh, Abel, I'm just so thrilled you're here! You can finally meet my brother. Let me make introductions!" Nina chirped, clearly still in hostess mode, but before she could, Vita cut across her.

"We don't have time for that now. Abel, do you have a key for this cell?"

"No," Abel answered flatly, managing the crippling disappointment of not getting a formal introduction to Nina's brother with aplomb. "But he does." He pointed at Strife's body with the torchiere he'd used to knock him out.

Vita squatted beside Strife, reaching out toward the reeking mass, and Winnie gasped.

"Vita, no!" she yelped, and Vita looked up quizzically. "You can't put your hands in his pockets! Didn't you see what came out of there?" Winnie's stomach heaved just thinking about the dead mouse, which was now likely a flatter, juicier version of itself somewhere under Strife's substantial body.

Vita heaved a belabored sigh that would have made Abel proud. "Who's going to do it then? You? Or do you want to wait for another alpaca to show up and ask him to take care of it?"

"Speaking of Gerald," Abel said without missing a beat. "You have him to thank for me being here to rescue you. He came to find me after he'd brought you here, but I couldn't get away from the walking cesspool there." He jerked a thumb at Strife's body. "And Gerald's a llama, actually," he added.

Vita had taken advantage of Winnie being distracted and was rooting through the folds of Strife's cloak, searching for pockets that might contain a keyring. She paused to look at Abel sardonically.

"He could be a unicorn for all I care. He could have helped us a lot more by bringing us straight here instead of leaving us to figure things out on our own."

Abel shook his head. "He doesn't know about this place. Very few individuals down here do. When Tod had this built, he—"

"Ha!" Nolan erupted from the sidelines, stopping Abel short and drawing all eyes.

He stomped over to stand before Tod, reaching up to wag a slender finger in his face.

"I knew it! I knew you'd built this thing!" He seemed to be on the brink of delivering a crushing blow, and Winnie felt a cheer rising in her that she'd have been mortified to admit to Verna. On a forgiving day, she might assume Tod had denied building the cell out of embarrassment or shame, but when she wasn't feeling so forgiving…

"*J'accuse!*" Nolan finally proclaimed.

Winnie closed her eyes and raised a hand to cover her face. She heard Vita mutter something unrepeatable, followed by the sound of continued searching. When she peeked out from under her hand at Nina, she was making a face that plainly said *he's doing his best.*

Tod was staring down at Nolan. "What?" he finally asked.

Nolan cleared his throat. "I said *j'accuse. J'accuse?*" he looked around questioningly.

Winnie foolishly failed to look away fast enough. "Winnie! Help me out here. You know what I mean, right?"

She uttered a few awkward sounds in response but was saved by Vita rising abruptly, flourishing a crusty, rough-hewn key.

"Both of you shut up," she said firmly, planting one sizeable foot on Strife's back and climbing over him to access the cell door.

Moments later, Nina burst out with Ren, wrapping Winnie in a tight hug before handing the toddler over.

Ren didn't speak; she just buried her face in Winnie's neck and clung to her as her aunt, surreptitiously wiping tears from under her sunglasses, whispered into her ear, "I missed you, Ren. I was so worried about you. I'm so happy to have you back in my arms, sweet girl."

Winnie breathed in her little girl scent, pressing her nose against Ren's temple to block out the putrid funk of Strife's still-unconscious body at their feet.

Unbidden, snatches of the dream she'd had of herself and Ren in the fast-growing tree invaded her thoughts. She shivered at the image of the spreading branches, of the haunting darkness that loomed below and the blinding light that hovered above. With effort, she forced the images from her mind and recited an incantation to herself instead: *now that I have you back, I'll never let you go again.*

"Winnie." She heard Tod's voice and cringed. She was going to have to let go of Ren sooner than she wanted to after all.

Handing the girl over to her father and turning away to give them privacy, she moved closer to Vita and Abel, who were watching the reunions playing out before them with impatience—Vita—and uninterest—Abel.

"What happens now?" she asked Vita.

"Now we leave. The most important thing is to get everyone out of the Depths as soon as possible. Preferably before this one wakes up." She aimed a lazy kick at her father's backside. "Since we don't know how much time we have before that happens, we need to wrap up the waterworks and get out of here."

Abel looked at Vita as if seeing her for the first time. "I like you," he said, and Winnie felt her eyebrows rise.

Vita looked down at the shorter man impassively. "Most people do." Then, she put two fingers in her mouth and whistled briefly. Silence fell immediately, and she nodded at her brother. "Grab a hand. We're locking him in."

Tod handed his daughter to Nina and joined Vita in hauling their father into the vacant cell, grunting and swearing with the effort. Finally, they dropped his arms, stepped around him and out of the cell, and closed the heavy door behind them. Tod turned the key in the lock and dropped it into his pants pocket.

"Don't lose that key," Vita warned him. "The last thing we need is for him to escape before we can get back down here to deal with him."

Tod looked at her darkly and nodded.

"Don't worry," he assured her. "I'll take care of it."

With Abel in the lead, it didn't take long for the larger party to make it out of the wraith compound and back onto the path Gerald had brought them down. They moved a little more slowly with Ren in tow, but despite being anxious to get back to the living world, Winnie found that she wasn't particularly afraid anymore. They had Ren back—her pudgy arms half-strangling Winnie as she rode on her back—and Nina was safe. Whatever the conflict with Strife may be, it would be easier to fight now that there was so much less at risk. Winnie couldn't help feeling that it wasn't really her fight to fight anyhow: Strife was Vita and Tod's father, not hers. She'd get her loved ones out of the crossfire, and then it would be their mess to sort out without her. That thought, along with the look she imagined on Verna's face when they reappeared with Renata, buoyed her spirits and her steps. She had no clue how much time would prove to have passed since they came over, but she felt no strain of fatigue. She coasted along on the satisfying cloud of a task accomplished.

Against her neck, Ren burbled forth a stream of information about her time in the cell with Nina, and Winnie listened attentively, gasping or chuckling or cooing at all the bits that seemed most important.

"...an' Nina tole me stories, Annie Woo. They were better'n Papa's stories, except when Papa talks about lava 'cause I like lava. You like lava too, Annie Woo. That's yours and my's favorite rock. It's prolly Nina's favorite rock too, but she didn't tell me stories about rocks. She tole me stories about people who are really animals an' about you an' her going through the dark an' coming out the door an' about selling ice cream. Nina's favorite ice cream is bumpy road. You ever had bumpy road ice cream, Annie Woo? When we get home, I'm gonna have Mommy take you an' me an' Nina for bumpy road ice cream, but I'm gonna tell them not to put any nuts in mine 'cause I don't like nuts in ice cream. Do you like nuts in ice cream, Annie Woo?"

Winnie grinned. "I sure do, little bug. Maybe we should try it the way—"

"I wanna have whipped cream and sprinkles on my ice cream and you and Mommy and Nina can have nuts on your bumpy road, okay?"

"Okay, it's a deal," Winnie put in briefly. Like her mother, Ren was generally in a mood either to talk or to listen, rarely both.

"I'm excited to get ice cream and to see Mommy and to give Butter Bear a big squeeze," Ren continued.

"I'm sure Butter Bear has missed you," Winnie agreed.

"It's okay that Butter Bear din't come here. He wouldna liked it." Ren fell silent, and Winnie held her breath, waiting for her niece to continue.

"He wouldna liked the bad man," she finally whispered, and Winnie felt a surge of mingled emotions: fear on Ren's behalf, gratitude toward Nina, and rage at Strife.

"You don't have to be afraid of that bad man anymore, Ren. We all came here just to rescue you. Now that we have you, we're going to keep you safe."

"Nina kep' me safe, Annie Woo. Nina brushed my hair and sleeped on the bed with me the whole time I sleeped, not like Mommy does when she says she's gonna sleep with me an' then gets up an' sleeps in her bed. And Nina tole me you were coming an' we just had to wait for you."

"She did?" Winnie asked, whispering because she found she suddenly couldn't get words out around the tightness in her throat.

"Nina tole me you comed and got Mommy when she was in trouble an' you were gonna come for her an' me too. I tole Nina she's my best friend an' she said I'm her best friend an' I said I can't be 'cause you're her best friend an' she said people can have as many best friends as they have love for. Nina has lots of love, Annie Woo, so you an' me can both be her best friend. Okay?"

Winnie was glad the girl's head leaned against her own so that she could feel Winnie's nod; Winnie had no words even for agreement. Instead, she communicated silently to the powers that be, sending out an unspoken message of intense, enduring gratitude too great to be articulated aloud.

Ren lapsed into silence, and Winnie trod along contentedly for some time, but that contentment deflated somewhat when Nolan's raised voice reached her.

"I hope you have a plan B in place, buddy, because my sister isn't coming back down here ever again."

Winnie peeked around Vita and Tod, who walked side-by-side in front of her, to look at Nolan. He'd turned to walk backward, keeping up with Abel and Nina, but clearly intent on facing Tod and making his stand there and then.

"Nina took the position voluntarily. She and I will work something out," Tod answered.

It was clear from Nolan's face that he was not having any of it.

"No. Period. Find someone else to do your job while you play house. My sister is done."

Winnie could see Tod's shoulders rising, and Nina must have sensed the same tension because she jogged past Abel to spin her brother around and whisper animatedly in his ear.

Winnie couldn't make out what they were saying, but knowing Nina, she was peacekeeping, trying to smooth things over in a way that would keep everyone happy.

Good luck with that, Winnie thought wryly, but she smiled nonetheless, knowing that regardless of the decisions Nolan and Tod thought they might be making on her behalf, Nina would certainly get her way in the end.

"Annie Woo?" Ren said quietly in Winnie's ear. "Wass that?"

Winnie looked around, but she saw nothing unusual. Well, there seemed to be an office building in the middle of a redwood forest off in the distance, and she didn't remember the volcano from the first time they'd come this way, but aside from this typical strangeness, she saw nothing unusual.

"What's what, little bug?" she asked. "What are you looking at?"

"Listen, Annie Woo." A sticky hand wrapped around Winnie's mouth to silence her, and she paused, straining her ears to hear what Ren was hearing.

After a few beats, Ren whispered, "Hear it?"

Winnie shook her head, and Ren's hand dropped away from her mouth. "No, baby, I don't hear—"

She broke off, turning her head slightly and focusing. She *did* hear something, a muffled thumping sound in the distance back the way they'd come.

She turned to hiss at Vita to stop, and Vita, breaking away from the group as it carried on ahead, jogged back to meet her.

"What is it?"

"Listen," Winnie instructed, and they both fell silent again. The thudding was definitely getting closer. "Hear that?"

Vita didn't answer, but Winnie easily read the tension in her face as she began scanning the road behind them where it disappeared over a small rise.

Vita's eyes settled in one spot, and Winnie followed her gaze. Within moments, a shaggy head appeared over the rise, quickly followed by the neck, body, and spastic, galloping legs of Gerald.

"Horsy!" Ren trilled over Winnie's shoulder.

"Don't let him hear you say that," Winnie told her distractedly. "What's he saying, Vita? Can you hear?"

Gerald was yelling as he ran, but his jostling, discombobulated gait cut off his words.

Vita squinted her eyes in concentration, and then swore under her breath. She turned to Winnie, her eyes flashing.

"Run," she breathed. Then she looked past Winnie to where the others had stopped to wait. "Run!" she called more urgently, and Winnie felt a prickle of dread creep up her spine at the fear in Vita's voice.

"What is it, Vita? What's he saying?" Winnie was already starting to jog toward the others.

"He's coming," Vita breathed, taking off ahead of Winnie. "Strife is out, and he's coming!"

Twenty-Five

Winnie whipped Ren off of her back, swinging the little girl over her hip and clutching her to the front of her body. She murmured reassurances in Ren's ear until her breath ran out, and then she simply held tight to her and focused on keeping up with the others.

Thanks to his impressive stride, Tod was far ahead of Winnie; she focused on his back, determined to catch up. But despite her previous buoyancy, the strain of running from the Nights and the long walk with Gerald to the hidden doorway began to make itself known. Determination wasn't enough to keep her on her feet, and with a cry, she stumbled forward, throwing out one hand to prevent Renata from hitting the ground. She heard a pop, and pain shot like fire up her arm.

Hearing her cry, both Tod and Vita skidded to a halt and pivoted to look back at where Winnie and Ren had fallen. Gerald caught up with their group just then, and Winnie felt his snuffling snout burrowing under one arm to prod her to her feet.

"I'll bring them!" he shouted to the siblings. "Get to the door and open it!"

Tod nodded and took off, but Vita, a look of doubt flitting briefly across her face, closed the distance between herself and the ruminant.

"Let me help," she panted, and she grabbed Winnie under her arms and heaved until she was back on her feet. Linking her fingers into a step, she hoisted both Winnie and Ren up onto Gerald's back.

"Thank you, Vita!" Winnie huffed as she struggled to regain her breath, but Vita wasn't paying attention. Her deep brown eyes, uncannily wide and fixed, were locked on something behind them.

"Go, Gerald! Go! Go!" she shouted, whacking the llama's haunch once and sprinting after the rest of the group, who were now cresting a hill in the middle distance.

The llama's jackrabbit takeoff nearly unseated Winnie, and she dug her fingers desperately into Gerald's furry neck, glancing down at Ren, who held tight to her aunt silently, her eyes wide with fear. Winnie uttered a few more reassuring whispers and tried her hardest to hold tight to Gerald. But the look on Vita's face refused to leave her mind, and even though every good instinct in her body told her not to, she finally cast a glance back over her shoulder to see their pursuer for herself.

In one powerful gust, the air left Winnie's lungs. An iridescent, roiling sea of insects pursued them. Billions and billions of tiny, segmented bodies, skittering legs, clicking mouthparts, and buzzing wings swarmed together in a tumbling, glittering mass, fresh bodies boiling up from underneath as the exhausted mass at the vanguard fell away. Curled corpses and used exoskeletons tumbled and rolled in the insect cloud's wake, abandoned by the moving ocean of pests.

And at their center, standing upright and unmoving as the insects in his thrall killed themselves to support his weight, rode Damion Strife.

Winnie inhaled a painful, gasping breath, tore her eyes away from the spectacle, and buried her face in Ren's hair. Even with her eyes closed, though, she could still see the loathsome, living sea that supported Strife, it's eerie, seamless motion like the inexplicable movement of a murmuration of starlings, it's chittering, crunching roar growing ever-louder behind them.

"Nearly…there…," she heard Gerald pant, and she opened her eyes. They were at the base of the hill the others had already disappeared over, and Winnie realized it must be the lip of the caldera they'd found themselves in when they'd passed through the door.

But they were getting to it awfully slowly. Winnie didn't dare look behind them again, but she could sense Gerald struggling to carry the weight of two passengers up the incline. They had to move faster.

"Gerald, let us down!" she called. "I can run from here!"

He didn't argue, and she felt his movements change under her as he pulled up, turning to the side so that she and Ren could jump off facing the hilltop with his form between them and the insectoid onslaught that wasn't slowing at all.

"Don't…look back…," Gerald huffed as she slid down, and Winnie didn't. She clutched Ren tightly and started moving the instant her feet hit the ground. But even her terror couldn't overwhelm her gratitude.

"Thank you…Gerald!" she shouted to him between breaths as he ran alongside her. "We owe…you…our lives!"

Perhaps Gerald would have been self-effacing in that moment and brushed off her thanks. Or perhaps he would have insisted it was his duty, or a favor to his friend Abel, who had done much for him as well, but Winnie didn't get to hear his response.

As they crested the hill, Gerald, clumsy and dysregulated from exhaustion, lost his footing and sprawled over the lip of the caldera, his back legs on the grassy hilltop and his front legs hanging over the steep drop down into the crater.

Winnie's momentum was too great to stop, and she traversed the lip and began slipping down the rocky incline they'd struggled to climb up when Gerald had first met them. In the dusty, painful confusion of stumbling and sliding down the side of the great crater, she tried to call out to Gerald, tried to look back to see if he was regaining his feet and following her, tried even to stop her downward trajectory to go back and help him, but the sounds of the others shouting and crying out told her all she needed to know about the likelihood of rescuing him.

When Winnie finally reached the bottom, struggling to keep her footing, Nolan and Nina rushed to support her as she scrubbed dust from her sunglasses and raked her hair out of her face.

She spun to look back for Gerald, babbling incoherently that they needed to go back, needed to help him the way he'd helped them…

But as she watched, she knew it was too late. In the confusion, she faintly picked out Vita's voice screaming for her to go through the door now, now,

now! But she couldn't look away from Gerald, whose watery brown eyes stayed fixed on hers as he gave up trying to pull himself off the ledge.

Thank you, she mouthed, and though she would never have thought a llama capable of smiling, she felt sure he was in his way.

Then the hoard rose up behind him, and in the blink of an eye, his form was lost under the clicking, black mass as it poured over the ledge and trickled down into the crater.

Winnie shrieked in horror, staring in frozen disbelief at the spot where Gerald had fallen. As she watched, a slit formed in the mass of insects, and a single spark of pure, white light rose through the seething mass to hover in the air above it. It pulsed once, and then it blinked out of existence.

Winnie squeezed her eyes closed, and tears she hadn't felt carved clean paths in the dirt on her cheeks. Someone was pulling her toward the door, and someone was talking to her, saying it was time to go. Still she stared, transfixed and shocked and certain that Gerald wasn't...That he hadn't just...

"Don't cry, Annie Woo." Ren's little voice broke through Winnie's trance, and she looked down at her niece, who had twisted herself around in her aunt's grasp to watch Gerald's last moments. "The horsy had to go on."

Winnie drew back, studying her niece's serene face.

"He did?" she asked, and Ren nodded, resting her head against her aunt's shoulder, as if nothing remarkable at all had happened to them in the last several minutes.

"...and we can't wait any longer!" Vita's voice was suddenly loud in her ear.

"What?" Winnie said lamely, and Vita grabbed her arm painfully.

"Welcome back. Go through the door, now!" Vita shouted into her face.

Winnie turned to face the door, where Nina and Nolan stood waiting for her to take Ren through. Abel stood behind Nina, watching Strife's movement down the steep hillside.

Winnie jumped into action, hope and relief working like a salve on her shaking legs and throbbing arm.

This is almost over! We just have to step through the door, and we're safe!

She ducked her head and made for the door, just as the skittering of the insects abated behind her. Strife had reached the floor of the caldera.

From behind her, she heard his malevolent chuckle, and she stopped in her tracks. Around the door, tiny hillocks of sand began to form, rising up from the cracked crater floor until they burst open like festering pustules. From within them rushed a small tide of creeping things that scaled the door frame.

Nolan made a choking sound, and Nina threw her hand out as if to hold the door, but Nolan pulled her back before she could get close to the insects. The three of them watched in horror as the film of insects poured up and over the frame, forcing the door closed with the sickening crunch of crushed bugs.

Twenty-Six

Silence settled in the great crater. The insects, those who had survived the terrible burden their master had placed on them, burrowed back into the ground or flew off over the crater's lip, indifferent to the drama their service and sacrifice had initiated on the caldera's floor.

Strife looked at the group assembled before him, and the group looked back. Winnie held tight to Ren, watching the monstrous man warily. No one moved. No one spoke.

Finally, after the last living, squirming things had faded back to the places insects hide, and the only sound to be heard was the buzzing of the predator's attendant flies and the ragged breathing of the assembled prey, Strife began to move.

He took one step forward, the frail husks of his servants crunching nauseatingly under his foot. Winnie felt her gorge rise again at the sound, but it had a very different effect on Abel. Scrambling comically on the loose soil, he scurried around Nina to the door, turning its knob and pressing against it exactly the way he had only minutes before.

Unlike then, it didn't budge.

Frantically, he rattled the knob, looking back over his shoulder once to where Strife continued to press closer. Finally, he turned slightly and threw his weight against it, rebounding with a painful-sounding *thunk* that sent him stumbling back against Nolan. When the younger man had helped him up, Abel turned to him and shook his head, fear deepening the dark shadows under his eyes.

"I can't open it," he whispered, and the hairs on Winnie's arms prickled to life. She'd never heard Abel sound the way he did in that moment.

He's afraid, she thought. *He's so close to giving up.*

Winnie closed her eyes and breathed deeply. There had to be a way out of this. If this was the last moment they'd share, she wasn't afraid for herself or for Tod and Vita. They'd lived lifetimes already, and the universe had systems in place for replacing them if the worst happened.

But she thought of Ren, wrapped tightly in her arms, and how little life she'd had. She couldn't let Strife harm her beautiful niece.

And, perhaps worse, if these really were their last moments of life, then she had to talk to Nolan and Nina one last time.

I owe them apologies. They wouldn't be here if I hadn't brought them. If they die here today, it's because I endangered them, not once, but twice.

Winnie opened her eyes and felt them prickle with tears. She was thankful for the sunglasses that still hid her unsettling new eyes from Ren, thankful that they hid her tears now. She couldn't bear for Nina to see them and mistake them for surrender.

Fury rose in her so quickly and completely that she hardly knew she was moving until she found herself in front of Nina. She unwrapped Ren's arms from around her neck and turned the girl's small body toward Nina, who gathered her up without question.

"Stay with Nina for a bit, okay?" she whispered against Ren's cheek, and the girl's blonde curls bobbed as she nodded her response.

"Winnie, use your powers!" Nina hissed over the top of Ren's head. "Do what you did the last time we were in a pickle!"

Winnie felt hysterical laughter burble in her throat, but she fought it down, frightened of how it would sound to Renata. But she still smiled weakly at her friend.

"In a pickle? Nina, you're the only person I know who would say that when we're so close to...," She trailed off, not knowing how she could finish that sentence without scaring Ren. "I just love you, Nina. There's no one in the world like you, and I'm so thankful you've been by my side through all this."

Nina smiled and pushed her glasses up the bridge of her nose. "Oh, Winnie! I love you, too!"

Winnie squared her shoulders. "I have to face this on my own this time. Mom and Dad knew where we were the last time because I'd used my magic, and a lot of it. There's not a drop of water in this crater, and without a guarantee they'd find us...I won't leave you and Nolan and Ren in the line of fire while I hope for a miracle."

Nina gave her a reassuring head bob, and Winnie turned to face Strife.

"Open the door," she said, her voice less tremulous than she'd expected but hardly commanding. "We're leaving."

"No," Strife answered, "you're not." A fly landed next to his eye, and Winnie found it immeasurably irksome that he made no move to swat it away.

"What you're going to do is hand me back that little girl you've got there," he told Winnie, his voice like hot gravel on bare feet and his black eyes keen and focused.

"Why?" Winnie asked, and Strife paused, clearly expecting another refusal rather than a question about his motives.

"Why?" he repeated. "Why do I want the offspring of an Elemental and a Fundamental?" He smiled at her, and Winnie twitched with revulsion at the sight. Several of his teeth were missing, and the ones that remained were rotted. Between the jagged, black lumps, bloody sockets oozed scarlet pus. Winnie dragged her eyes away from the putrescent sight, focusing on Strife's eyes and nothing else.

"That little girl is a marvel, a being of unknown power. Imagine," he said, his pitiless eyes flaring with sudden desire. "Imagine what she'll be capable of. Imagine what she could be made to do in the right hands..."

"Yeah, that's not going to happen." Vita's voice caught both Winnie and Strife by surprise, but it was nothing compared to their shock when she hurdled her body, full-force, into Strife's. The big man was knocked off his feet, and Vita somersaulted over him, regaining her footing as she slowed and spun to confront her father. Strife was a big man, and he reeked of ill-health, but Winnie was taken aback by how quickly he too was back on his feet and facing Vita.

"Think you're ready to take on your old man, do you?" he taunted her, his putrefactive leer at odds with his hunched, defensive posture.

A glint caught Winnie's eye, and she realized with horror that Strife had pulled a knife from somewhere in his voluminous robes.

"Vita! He has a knife!" Winnie shouted.

"I see it!" Vita answered. "Find a way to open that door while I deal with this piece of—"

Before she could finish her sentence, Strife was on her, and Winnie backed up fearfully as father and daughter—and mortal enemies—met in a lashing, violent embrace. Strife swung the short knife in great arcs, but Vita, quicker-footed and more agile, leapt this way and that to avoid his blows. She was clearly at a disadvantage without a weapon of her own, but she drew Strife's full attention, and Winnie knew she had to take advantage of his distraction.

She turned to the door, trying the handle again in desperation.

"Maybe it opens from the other side," Nina suggested tensely, her eyes glued to the imbalanced battle.

Winnie nodded, rushing around the back of the door. But when she reached for the knob, she found there wasn't one: it was simply the other side of the door, flat and remarkable only for its missing knob.

"Nothing. There's nothing there," she reported when she came back around to stand beside Nina. "There's no way to do this!" Winnie heard the frustration in her voice, but she couldn't stop herself from losing patience. They'd come so far for their rescue to fail here!

Furious, she dug the fingers of both hands into her hair, knocking the sunglasses askew. "Ugh! Stupid things," she howled, snatching them off of her face and cramming them into her pocket. She sighed in frustration.

"Winnie?" Nina said from beside her. "Winnie, look…"

Winnie followed Nina's gaze to the doorknob. It was glowing.

Winnie's head snapped up, and she looked at Nina. Nina's mouth fell open as she looked into Winnie's face.

"Winnie!" she gasped. "Your eyes!"

Nolan had watched this exchange anxiously, and he scooted behind his sister, craning his head over her shoulder to look at Winnie.

"Oh, wow," he marveled. "Winnie, your eyes are…," he let the sentence trail away.

"Are what? What are my eyes?" The sounds of the continuing fight between Vita and Strife filled the space between them, and Winnie made a circling motion with her hands to hurry the siblings' answers along.

"They're kind of…sparkly, Winnie," Nina finally breathed. "Right, Nole?"

"Yeah," he answered, still staring. "Glowing."

Winnie looked back at the door, but a small hand on her arm distracted her. She looked back to see Ren, who had until that moment been distracted by the cat-and-mouse fight behind them, staring at her intently.

"Open the doe, Annie Woo," she said, her sweet, soft consonants warming Winnie's heart.

Winnie reached out and clutched the knob, uttering a beseeching whisper as she turned it and pushed it open.

Nolan crowed, and Nina turned Ren to thrust her hurriedly into Winnie's arms.

"Take her now, Win! I'll hold it open for Tod and Vita. We'll be right behind you!"

"No!" The sudden shout from behind them startled both women, and they turned to face Strife, who had paused in his attacks on Vita to stare at the open door.

Winnie met his gaze fearlessly, and his black eyes grew microscopically larger as he regarded her.

"A Night-touch?" he muttered in bewilderment, and though Winnie had no clue what that meant or why it mattered, she could tell he was distraught over the discovery.

"Go through the door, Winnie!" Vita shrieked, struggling on shaking legs to regain the group.

With a deftness that beggared belief, Strife closed the space between himself and his exhausted daughter and lashed out one great, filthy fist. It connected with her temple with a sickening *whump*, and Vita toppled unceremoniously to the dirt.

"Vita!" Winnie shrieked, but Nina held her back.

"You have to go through! Nolan and I will get her! Just go, Winnie!"

Nina didn't wait for a response. She wheeled around to attend to Vita, but her progress was stopped in an instant.

Tod stood before her, blocking her route to Vita. With one large hand, he clutched her by the shoulder, and with the other, he slid Strife's knife between her ribs.

Twenty-Seven

Fog rolled over Winnie's brain when the blade of the knife disappeared into Nina's fragile, mortal flesh.

Frozen, Winnie watched as Nina gaped at Tod in disbelief, silent shock twisting her expression into an incredulous mask.

He withdrew the knife, watching coldly as Nina slid from his grip and slumped to the ground, her brother already kneeling at her side. Winnie saw Nolan's mouth moving as he grappled with Nina's limp body, saw his hand searching her ribcage, clutching tightly when it found the hot, wet wound, uselessly attempting to stanch the flow of blood.

Winnie looked at Nina's face, white now, her bluish lips still distorted by surprise. Her brown eyes peered up at Nolan's face. Her glasses had been knocked askew as she collapsed, and Winnie had the irrational urge to straighten them.

She found her feet moving then, carrying her to her friend's side. She knelt on the dirt, her arms still wrapping the silent, still Ren in a protective hug. She reached out for Nina's glasses with her unhurt hand, but when she looked at Nina's eyes, she knew there was no point. Nina wouldn't need them any longer.

With a *whoosh* like gushing water, the fog in Winnie's mind cleared, and suddenly she heard all there was to hear at once: Nolan's choking, breathless sobs as he cradled his sister's body, Vita's confused murmurs as Abel prodded her back to consciousness, Abel's sedate snuffling as he processed the shock and pain of his friend's demise…and one other sound, one that Winnie turned her head to catch more of, thankful in some remote, distant way that the pain of losing Nina hadn't set in yet—though she knew that keeping it at bay now would have terrible consequences for her later.

Tod and Strife, complacent in their victory, huddled together in fervent whispering, taking advantage of the chaos of the scene as Vita and Abel moved to attend to Nina's prostrate form. Winnie kept her head bowed over her niece in apparent grief, but her focus stayed firm on the Fundamentals' heated debate.

"…didn't have to leave it until the last minute. It was foolish, old man. You could have done away with her at any time." Tod reprimanded Strife.

"And do what with the kid? Bounce it on my knee? Do you think I came here to babysit while you took your time luring your sister down here?"

"Well, as you can see, *Father*, there were complications I had to deal with." Tod spat out the honorific like a profanity. "I assumed it would be just me and Vita coming back here, and the story would hold. How was I supposed to know my darling sister-in-law and her moronic boyfriend would show up to save the day?

"You're the one who's screwed this up. Vita would be locked in that cell right now if you hadn't gotten yourself knocked out by a one-hundred-fifteen-pound wraith. How am I going to convince the Elementals she orchestrated this whole thing if she escapes to implicate me? If you'd managed to get that part right—"

"Watch what you say to me, boy." Strife's growling voice sounded suddenly dangerous. "This is all your doing. We should have snatched the baby the minute it was born, like I wanted—"

"That wouldn't have worked, you old fool! The family already didn't like me; they would have suspected me. Do you have any idea how hard I had to work to wheedle my way in with those idiots? How hard it was to earn their trust? We can keep the child here without starting a war with the Elementals! This can still work.

"We'll close the door again and kill the mortals. Lock up the other two. When I go back alone, they won't question my story. I'll still tell them Vita planned it all and that she's on the run. I narrowly escaped with Winnie and the girl, but tragically we got separated in the Liminus, and they're gone. The child will be here where we can train her, and they won't know she lived until it's too late. Once we know what her powers are, we can leverage them against the Others. There will be nothing to stop us..."

"*Nothing to stop us*?" Strife's voice seethed with condescension. "There's one problem with your plan, boy: you never mentioned the little Elemental had been Night-touched!" Strife's clearly fought to control his fury. His flies' insectoid buzzing increased with his agitation.

"What difference does that make?"

"Stupid, stupid boy! I should never have left your education up to your mother!" Venom laced Strife's hissing whisper. "You really know nothing about this place."

"Don't take too much credit, old man," Tod hissed.

Strife chuckled, but it was a cruel, mirthless sound that made Winnie shiver.

"If I hadn't shown up when I did to explain how things really work, you'd have killed that Elemental in that cage. And what good would that have done you, hmm?"

Tod didn't respond to this, and Winnie had to fight the urge to look up at his expression.

"You didn't know what you were talking about then, and you don't now, either. Try closing the doors on that one! Try keeping her locked up here! The Nights and all their powers are contained, but she's taken some of that now. Kill her before she figures out what that power can do. Before we all do! Kill her, and we'll figure out how to handle the Others' Inquiry after she's dead." Strife's malevolent hiss was nearly lost in the frantic buzzing of his hoard, but it still struck a chord somewhere deep in Winnie.

Tod's patience had apparently run out. "What are you talking about? If she tries to open another door, we'll just close it again."

In a low voice that Winnie strained with all her might to hear, Strife muttered an answer that solidified her resolve. "We may not be able to if she prevents it."

"We need to go now," she whispered frantically to the gathered mourners, and Nolan's eyes rose in a daze.

"We can't leave her here," he mumbled. "We can't outrun them in there." He didn't have to explain who *them* was; Winnie knew he was thinking of the Nights that lurked in the darkness beyond the open door.

"We have to try. You have to carry her. And we have to move fast. If I opened that door, then I can close it, and I think I can keep it closed."

"They'll be on us before we all make it through," Nolan lamented. Winnie could see that she wasn't getting through to him. She searched his face frantically for a way to convince him to trust her.

"You could if they were distracted," Abel said beside him, and Winnie had barely opened her mouth to protest before he clambered to his feet and turned to face Strife and Tod.

"Abel!" Winnie cried out, but he ignored her. The thought of losing Abel after having lost Nina threatened to dislodge the crushing mound of grief that she'd managed to keep at bay. He was going to sacrifice himself for her, for them!

No, not for us. For Nina. He's going to sacrifice himself so that Nina can go back where she belongs.

She added the terrible weight of his kindness to her catalogue of grief and endeavored to feel it, all of it, when Ren was safe at home once more.

Abel squared his bony shoulders and made his stand.

"I'm going to tell everyone what you did here, Tod!" Abel shouted at his longtime boss. "I've been here a long time, and I'm going to make sure every new essence that comes down here knows what the two of you have done!"

Strife and Tod stared at Abel in disbelief, an infuriating hint of humor twisting up Tod's lip. Winnie stared at him with disgust, but her ears were tuned not to Abel but to Vita, who was murmuring hushed instructions to her two companions.

"I'm going to keep doing my job because it's my job, but I'm not going to be pleasant about it like I usually am!" Abel shouted, and Winnie hoped Vita understood how quickly they needed to move; Abel didn't have much leverage, and the little he had was running out.

She needn't have worried: with a shout like a whipcrack, Vita signaled their departure. Rising as one, she and Nolan hefted Nina's body, slinging it over Nolan's shoulder as both he and Winnie darted for the door.

With a furious screech, Strife commanded his son, "Stop them! Kill them! Don't let them get through the door!"

The reek of ozone instantly filled the air, and Winnie felt electricity gather on her skin. Strands of Ren's hair rose before her face. Tod was gathering his magic.

Winnie didn't look back, and she didn't stop. She pitched headlong through the door with Ren, Nolan and Nina's body following close behind. She stumbled in the blackness beyond, and dropped to her knees, twisting to scramble back to grab the doorknob. In a tumbling mass that seemed too big for one person, Vita fell through as well, nearly knocking Winnie off-balance. The last sight of the Depths Winnie saw before she yanked the door closed by its glowing knob was Tod's pale face, contorted by rage, and a ball of white fire speeding toward her from his outstretched hands.

Twenty-Eight

Holding the knob with all her might, Winnie commanded the door to stay locked. The knob glowed red momentarily, and she felt the skin on her palm sear, but still she held tight, unwilling to let the heat from Tod's parting volley prevent her from locking this door against them.

The flare of heat quickly abated, and the knob shone once more with warm, white light. She pressed her other hand against its wood surface and whispered another command, directing the bright white connection she felt flowing through the knob in the same way she directed her powers when autumn turned to winter. Gradually, the white light suffusing the knob faded, and when she finally removed her hand from it, it was scarcely visible in the murky darkness. As ever, the only light in this liminal space now came from the crack beneath the door.

Winnie fell back, panting from fear and effort. The pain in her arm, forgotten during their chaotic exodus, returned as a dull, nagging ache.

"We should test it," Vita's voice said in the darkness, and though the thought terrified Winnie, she knew Vita was right. She stepped aside, her raw, burnt palm aching as a chubby hand grasped hers.

"You okay, little one?" she asked Ren, and when she looked down at Ren's face, she was surprised to see that it was dimly visible.

"Annie Woo, your eyes are shiny," Ren informed her, and when she looked up at Vita for confirmation, the tall woman raised her eyebrows.

"Yep," she said. "She's right. They glow. Like one of those weird, deep sea fish."

"That's so…," Winnie said, unsure how to finish the sentence.

"Freaky? Yes. It's helpful right now, I'll give you that, but you're definitely going to want to get some colored contacts or something when we get aboveground again."

"Thanks," Winnie said sardonically, stooping to sweep Ren up into her arms. Her back and shoulders groaned at the strain, but she wasn't about to let go of this precious bundle when she'd already lost so many people: Gerald and Nina and now…

"Poor Abel," she said into the dimness. "He was so much better than I gave him credit for."

"I beg your pardon?" came a voice in the darkness, and Winnie spun in shock in the direction she thought it came from.

"Abel?"

"I think I proved myself before today, thank you very much," he said tetchily, and Winnie groped with her free, unburnt hand in the darkness that her glowing eyes only slightly illuminated until she found the gaunt, slumped form of the steward.

"Oh, Abel! I thought Tod…I mean I thought he had…"

"Tried to destroy me? He did. Your mighty lady-warrior snatched me back through the door by my hood."

"*Mighty lady-warrior?*" Vita said in the darkness, but Winnie thought she heard a note of pride under the skeptical tone.

"Speaking of which," Abel carried on as if he hadn't been interrupted. "You need to reopen the door and let me back through."

"Hell no," Winnie and Vita said in unison.

"I don't belong here," Abel insisted. "You have to leave me in the Depths."

"That isn't going to happen, Abel. I'm not reopening that door, and I'm not leaving you to face Tod."

"Winnie, you're not hearing me—"

"I'm hearing you, Abel. But I'm overriding you. You're coming with us. Vita, you've got Nolan's hand?"

"Yep. We're with you."

With that, she grabbed Abel's hand and, ignoring his increasingly frantic protestations, began marching, keeping her back to the door in the hopes of moving in a straight line.

They'd made it only a few steps before the piercing screeches of the Nights drowned out all sound. Ren tensed against Winnie's body, and Winnie felt her hands fly up to her head. Winnie wished she could cover her ears as well, but she refused to let go of Abel, who had stopped dead at the sound.

"I told you!" he cried out over the horrible wailing. "They know I'm here! They don't let the dead leave the Depths!"

Panic flooded Winnie's body. Why had she been so insistent? Why hadn't she listened when Abel fought leaving the protection of the doorway?

She could hear Nolan moaning behind her, and she cursed herself doubly. Nolan had suffered the worst of the Nights' attack the first time they'd passed through. How could he withstand another barrage, especially now that he had Nina's body to carry as well?

In the dim light cast by her eyes, Winnie saw the darkness begin to swirl, and a gusting wind picked up around them, carrying shrieks in all directions as the Nights encircled them.

"Close your eyes and scream!" she heard Vita command as she had last time. Winnie tipped her head back and wailed, channeling all of the grief, anger, betrayal, and frustration at having made it so far only to fail in the last few moments.

And that was when Ren started to glow.

Twenty-Nine

The sudden appearance of Ren's warm, white light shocked Winnie into silence, and it seemed to have the same effect on the Nights because instantaneously and utterly, silence fell around them.

Around them, but not among them. While Winnie and the Nights fell silent, Nolan persisted in shrieking hoarsely with his eyes closed until Vita, her eyes also squeezed tightly shut, said his name a few times. Gradually, he calmed, and Winnie heard her whisper to him to stay calm and quiet and to not, under any circumstances, open his eyes.

Winnie had never bothered to close hers. She'd already seen what there was to see of the Nights, and she was too anxious to get through the Liminus with Ren to bother with being cautious. Now she gazed in awe at her niece whose skin glowed just enough to illuminate the six travelers, both living and not.

Ren was looking down at herself as well, apparently delighted by her new-found ability.

Her ability...of course! thought Winnie. *Her father is the steward of death, and her mother is the source of life each spring. Why shouldn't Ren have the space in between them?*

Renata looked up into her aunt's face. "Annie Woo, I'm a nightlight."

Despite the darkness, and the loss, and the burdens she'd have to face when they finally reemerged among the living, Winnie laughed.

"You sure are, Ren. We can use you to read bedtime stories."

The girl smiled sweetly, and Winnie felt warmth spreading through her limbs, easing the pains in her hand and arm and the soreness in her back, and renewing her spirits just enough to make the situation not completely hopeless.

"I think you're even taking away some of my ouchies, Ren!"

"Girl...no. That's me," Vita whispered behind her, and Winnie registered the hand on her shoulder.

"Oh. Duh," she responded, rolling her eyes in the semi-darkness.

"What's happening? Is it safe to open our eyes?"

"No, absolutely not," Winnie insisted. "I have no idea what's going on. They're still here, but they're just standing around us. Well, not *standing*, obviously..."

"Shut up."

Winnie snickered. Vita really was growing on her.

"So, what are they doing?"

"They're just..." Winnie looked around, trying not to hold her gaze in any one place too long. There was no way to differentiate one Night from the next; each mass of devastating emptiness blended with the next. "They're just...there."

"Annie Woo," Ren said, tugging at her aunt's shirt. "Go."

"Go where, sweet pea? I don't know where to..."

But suddenly she did know. She followed Ren's pointing finger. Ahead of them, the Nights drifted apart, forming a gap just the right size for the party of six to pass through.

"Vita? Do you have Nolan?"

"Yes, I've still got him."

"Abel, are you seeing what I'm seeing?"

Abel cleared his throat and mumbled something affirmative, apparently at an uncharacteristic loss for words.

"Okay, then," she said, squeezing Ren close. "Keep your eyes closed and hold tight to one another, everybody."

Winnie marched forward, following the path between the Nights with Ren's glow leading the way. Her free hand, its burns soothed by Vita's healing energy, held tightly to Abel's and his in turn to Vita's. Nolan followed them all, his limp hand grasped firmly by Vita's strong one, but if he felt regular pulses of healing warmth, he gave no indication. Rather, their silent progress was marked by his occasional, heart-breaking sobs.

Winnie's view of the path before them never changed as they walked. With each step, she saw only the shadowy darkness before them and the despairing, endless void of the Nights spreading off to either side, forming an unsettling corridor comprising absence and nothingness. She considered once or twice the folly of following a course laid by monsters of unendurable darkness, but something in Ren's relaxed demeanor reassured her. From time to time, Ren even yawned, laying her head on her aunt's shoulder, and Winnie wondered if she was so at peace that she was actually drifting off. So, she let Ren's comfort sooth her fears and kept walking without hesitation in the direction the Nights led her.

And then, when Winnie was beginning to wonder whether she would have to stop the whole party to move Ren to the other hip, a faint light appeared in the darkness.

"I see something," she reported back to Vita, and she heard Vita murmuring to Nolan in turn.

Winnie had to force herself not to move faster: if she was wilting under the weight of a three year old, she could only imagine how fatigued Nolan must be feeling as he dutifully carried Nina's lifeless form. Winnie marched steadily onward, her gaze glued to the light ahead of and above them. Gradually, its form became clearer, the liquid light shimmering and bluish like sunlight on water. Winnie pressed her lips together in grim remembrance: this is what the cemetery birdbath looked like from below. They would emerge from the same pool they'd entered through, but she felt poignantly how different she and Nolan would be from the people who had climbed down the watery stairs what seemed like a lifetime ago.

Perhaps even Vita, too, had been changed by what had happened before the open door back in the Depths. She and her brother clearly hadn't been close, but he had betrayed her in the cruelest way imaginable, endeavoring to imprison her to protect his ambition and greed and aligning himself with Strife, the Fundamental of destruction and decay. Perhaps when this was over,

Winnie would have the chance to ask Vita how she felt about it all. Perhaps they'd recover together, new friends forged by mutual loss.

Movement from above interrupted Winnie's thoughts, and she watched in fascination as the water above them swirled and stretched, growing wider as it descended from the circular aperture in the darkness. The Nights shifted to close the path before them, and Winnie stopped, calling back over her shoulder to the others to follow suit.

The water continued swirling, but liquid steps emerged within it, and Winnie tentatively put one foot on the first step. It felt as solid as wood. She stepped back down, urging Abel forward until he was on his way up the stairs before talking Vita and Nolan through their first steps. When they were all safely on the stairs and heading up, Winnie stepped up onto the stairway. She paused there, turning to scan the monsters that surrounded them.

"I...," she said into the darkness, but she didn't know what to say. She felt she should say something, but what?

Ren came to the rescue. Lifting her head sleepily from Winnie's shoulder, she waved a chubby hand at the creatures that surrounded them.

"Bye-bye. Love you!" she chirped gayly, and Winnie chuckled as she climbed the last few steps to the living world.

Thirty

Winnie emerged to find her friends blinking in the midday light. They had no way of knowing how long they'd been gone, but the air felt warm and springy as it had when they'd descended, so they hadn't been gone long enough for Verna to have passed the seasonal torch to Meri yet.

Nolan sat with his sister on the grass in the shade of the flowering crab tree's one leafy branch. He leaned against the trunk, cradling her head and shoulders. She looked otherworldly lying there in the truest sense of the word: her face was milky pale, including her lips, and her heavy inertness mocked the theatrical death of actors in films. Winnie sat down on the bench they'd used to climb into the birdbath with Tod and settled Ren beside her, watching from afar as Nolan spoke quietly to his sister. She wanted desperately to go to him, to put an arm around him and sit quietly with her friend for the last time, but she knew she belonged where she was, apart from the siblings. Nolan deserved this time to say goodbye to his sister. He hadn't had the opportunity with the threats of Tod and Strife hanging over them in the Depths and the exhausting slog through the Liminus in the dark, miserable space behind his closed eyelids. This was solitary time the two of them deserved.

Winnie heard a muffled cry, and she looked over to Vita and Abel. Vita stood silently watching the brother and sister, and Winnie's chest tightened when she imagined how Vita must feel watching Nolan mourn his sister. Her brother certainly would never cry over her this way.

Surprisingly, though, it had been Abel's stifled sob she'd heard. Standing with the sunlight behind him so that he seemed hazy around the edges, Abel looked at his friend, fat tears tracking down his jowly cheeks and dropping onto his rough tunic.

Winnie closed her eyes in shame for having pulled three of these people into this mess. They'd been involved only because of her, and she'd asked too high a price for their selflessness.

Movement beside her caught her eye. She would have expected Ren to have been asleep already after their long journey, but the girl's eyes, though heavy-lidded, were bright and attentive. They stayed fixed on Nina as she slid down the front of the bench and made to go to her.

"Ren, baby, stay with Annie Woo," Winnie urged her quietly, trying not to interrupt Nolan's silence.

Ren turned to her. "No, Annie Woo. I go by Nina now."

The girl's intention was delivered so matter-of-factly that Winnie said nothing and simply watched her go. She toddled over to where Nina lay. To Nolan's credit, he didn't try to stop her from climbing up onto Nina's lap.

Nolan watched her get settled and smiled feebly when she looked up into his face.

"Nina died," she informed Nolan, and though Winnie gasped and began scrambling to her feet to intervene, she stopped herself and sat back down when she saw the look of bemusement on Nolan's face.

"Yes," he said quietly. "She did."

"She should come back," Renata decided, and Nolan chuckled, but Winnie suspected it conveniently covered a sob.

"I agree, Ren," he told the girl. "I loved her very much, and think she should have lived much, much longer."

Winnie felt another stab of guilt and let it swamp her. She wanted to feel the pain of this now; she owed it to Nina. Tears prickled her tired eyes, and like Abel, she didn't bother to wipe them away.

Ren listened to Nolan wide-eyed, nodding her head in agreement.

"Okay," she said as if they'd negotiated a compromise on a difficult point of impasse.

"Okay," Nolan repeated with less certainty. Winnie shared his confusion: it seemed as though they *were* agreeing to something, but she wasn't sure what.

Ren hiked her leg up on Nina's belly so that she was turned to face her. She reached out for Nina's lifeless cheeks, grasping her slack face in her dimpled hands and looking intently at the woman who had cared for her during their frightening incarceration.

Before Winnie knew what was happening, Ren's hands began to glow.

"Ren?" Winnie called, jumping up from the bench and flying to Nina's side, her worried gaze fixed on her niece. "Ren, what are you doing?"

Nolan watched the girl in alarm, and Winnie realized how bizarre this must look. After all, his eyes had been tightly closed as they navigated the Night-lined path; he didn't see Ren's nightlight trick.

"Ren?" Winnie said again, but her niece neither let go of Nina's face nor acknowledged her aunt. Her attention stayed focused entirely on Nina, and Winnie watched in fearful fascination as the warm light Ren produced sent feelers of light down both sides of Nina's neck, disappearing momentarily under her tunic only to reappear on her arms and continue their paths down to her fingers.

Winnie felt her breath stop in her chest, and she glanced up at Nolan, whose opposite reaction had him drawing great, gasping breaths. Vita appeared suddenly beside him, grasping his shoulder. His breaths calmed, and he glanced up at her thankfully before snapping his eyes back to his sister's face.

Winnie didn't know if Nolan could feel the magic gathering around them, but Vita caught her eye. A look of burning determination passed between the women, and Vita grabbed Nina's lifeless hand in hers.

Winnie's powers were not nearly as useful as Vita's in this situation, but she closed her eyes and summoned her magic nonetheless. She wouldn't direct it, but she'd make it available for Ren, and perhaps that offering, even if it failed, would expiate a fraction of the great debt she owed her friend.

Nolan choked back a cry, and Winnie's eyes flew open. Where Ren's rosy hands met Nina's pallid skin, color was beginning to return. Gradually, it spread across Nina's face and down her neck. Winnie watched her hands, her pulse quickening when Nina's bluish nails regained their warm olive hue.

And then her eyes opened.

"Nina!" Nolan cried, dropping his forehead to meet his sister's and unleashing a fresh torrent of tears. Winnie felt her chest tighten, and she gathered Ren up into her arms when the girl finally pulled her hands away from Nina's face.

Nina blinked confusedly a few times before her eyes settled on Winnie's face. Thinking quickly in the way only a fellow spectacles-wearer would, Nolan dug her glasses out of his pocket and eased them onto her face. She looked up at him gratefully—if a bit uncomprehendingly—and then back at Winnie.

She smiled and was about to speak when Abel popped his head over the top of Winnie's.

"Abel!" Nina exclaimed, her look of surprise reminding Winnie hauntingly of the expression she'd worn at the moment of her death.

"Yes, Abel's here!" Winnie said joyfully.

Nina looked at her in confusion.

"And look, Nina: Nolan's here, and Vita—"

"That's wonderful, Winnie, really, but what about Abel?"

Winnie cocked her head to one side, sensing that she was missing something. "What about him?" She craned her head around to see him, but he was backlit by the sun still, and she could hardly make him out...

"Uh-oh," she said.

Abel wasn't hazy because of the sun, she realized. Abel was fading away.

Thirty-One

Winnie shifted Ren back into Nina's arms and jumped up. She reached out to touch Abel, but instead of feeling the firm, fleshy hand she'd held as she led him through the Liminus, she found a spongy simulacrum. Her fingers seemed to sink in before encountering resistance.

"Abel," she said, worry drawing her brows together. "What's happening?"

For once, Abel didn't seem to have an answer. He simply looked back at her and shrugged.

"I don't belong here. I'm not alive. This body isn't a real body, remember? It's just the idea of a body."

Winnie bit the side of her nail.

"I have to go back, Winnie. You have to reopen this door. I'll find my way."

"Please don't ask me to do that, Abel. I can't bear to have you go back there. What will happen if Tod destroys you? Will it be like…" She faltered, struggling to face this new peril without breaking down.

"Like Gerald?" he finished for her. "No, I'm afraid it won't be. Gerald passed on through mishap. It doesn't happen often, but it happens. I'll be destroyed by the Nights or by Tod himself; either way, my destruction will be punitive. There's no passing on after that."

"What is there?" Winnie was afraid of the answer, but she had to know.

Once again, though, Abel didn't answer. He smiled at her kindly and shook his head.

"I'm going back, Winnie. I have no choice. I can't stay here like this. It feels…wrong. And I'm afraid that if I keep fading, I'll be stuck here." He shuddered as he contemplated it. "I don't want to be just an essence with no form. I don't want to spend eternity in a world I don't belong in with people I can't talk to and who can't see me." Abel choked on this last part, and Winnie cringed at the thought of wandering among strangers forever, unseen and unheard, longing for an end that would never come.

"Let me spend the few minutes I have left before I go with my friend," he added.

Vita and Nolan had helped Nina to her feet and moved her gingerly to the bench, where she sat with Ren on her lap.

Winnie nodded to Abel and swiped a tear from her cheek. The least she could do was respect Abel's last wishes.

Abel sat down beside Nina, and the three other adults moved away to give them privacy. Nolan had a hard time looking away from his sister, but he turned to Winnie when she told him and Vita Abel's intentions.

"You can't let him go back there," he said emphatically, pushing his glasses up his nose. "It's suicide."

"He's already dead, Nolan," Winnie reminded him gently, but she knew what he meant. "Anyway, I think that may be the point. He'd rather take his chances with the Nights than face Tod. I don't blame him."

"I shouldn't have pulled him through the door," Vita lamented, and Winnie was touched by the candor in her voice.

"You did the right thing, Vita. He told us his story, Nina and me, when we were there the first time. It was sad. There was a reason he didn't have an anchor, a reason he didn't pass on a long time ago. He wasn't wanted, wasn't loved. Pulling him through with us showed him he may not have been wanted then, but he is now."

Vita looked away.

"Vita? Are you crying?"

"No. Shut up."

Winnie caught Nolan's eye, and he smiled sadly. "What is passing on, Winnie? What happens?"

"I don't know. Nina asked Abel that, and he told her she'd have to wait to find out. But I know it's good. It's the goal."

"It isn't fair. I know what he's done for Nina, how much he helped her all the time she was down there. He works around the clock. And he did the same for Tod. That bastard is going to repay him by…" Nolan bit his lip, unable to finish articulating the unfairness of the thought.

"He should pass on."

A phrase echoed through Winnie's mind: *She should come back.*

Winnie slapped her forehead, and the noise drew Ren's attention. Winnie motioned for the girl to come to her.

Ren scrambled down off of Nina's lap and ran to her aunt, who squatted down in the grass to whisper in her niece's ear. Ren listened intently to Winnie's words, and when Winnie drew back and asked if she understood, Ren grinned a sleepy smile and nodded. Then she walked back over to Abel and Nina, climbed up onto the bench between them, and spoke to Abel.

The three adults watched from afar as Abel embraced Nina, Ren's tiny body wedged in the space between them. Nina's face was lined with sorrow, but Abel's, though eerily transparent, looked younger and more serene than Winnie had ever seen it. With one arm still wrapped around his friend, he nodded to Ren, and she reached up confidently and placed her hand where his heart would be if he still had one.

He looked up then and met Winnie's eye, and he raised a hand to say goodbye, his droopy eyes drawing up at the sides with his smile. Winnie raised a hand in response, and though she expected another wave of crushing emotion, none came.

As Ren's hand once again began to glow, the look on Abel's face changed. His mouth opened slightly, and his smile gave way to a look Winnie couldn't quite name, though it made her heart swell with joy when she saw it.

In a moment, he was gone; a bright, glittering light flashed once where he had sat and then disappeared into thin air.

Epilogue

Winnie and Nolan, supporting Nina between them, stopped at the bottom of the stairs leading up to Nolan's front door. Nina unwound her arm from Winnie's so that she could turn to face her.

"I don't think I'll ever forget the look on Verna's face when she opened the door and saw Ren," she said with a careworn smile. The stress of the events she'd endured—being incarcerated, worrying over Ren, fighting their way out of the Depths, and, of course, being dead for a while—showed on her face: her cheeks looked hollow, and dark circles shadowed her eyes.

"I won't either," Winnie responded. She smiled too as the memory played out in her mind: Verna yanking open the door with such force that it banged against the wall stopper and startled the sleeping Ren into wakefulness. Ren had spun in Winnie's arms and, laying eyes on her weeping, wordless mother, she'd croaked out an exhausted but joyful "Mommy!"

Winnie and the others had watched silently as Verna scooped her daughter into her arms, clinging so tightly to the girl's tiny body that Ren squirmed.

"You mashin' me, Mommy."

Verna had smiled down at her daughter, pushing back her dirty curls and running her hands over Ren's face as if to reassure herself this really was her living daughter back in her arms.

"Thank you," Verna had whispered, still gazing down adoringly at her daughter's face. But then she looked up at the four exhausted, bloodied adults, and the color drained from her face.

She reached out for Winnie, pulling her into a hug that squashed Ren between them.

"Thank you, Winnie. Thank you for bringing her home to me," Verna murmured in Winnie's ear, and Winnie found herself temporarily lost for words. The little body between the sisters had begun to protest then, and Verna shifted her to one hip so that she could pull Winnie tighter against her. Winnie didn't object; she just held her sister and was held by her.

Even when Winnie felt she could speak again, she didn't. She stayed pressed silently against Verna's slender, strong body as a new knowledge sparked to life within her.

Before she could consider it, more urgent questions began queuing in her mind. What would come out when she finally had to speak? What could she possibly say to make what had happened feel manageable? How was she going to explain everything that had happened to her sister? Verna would hear the story of Tod's betrayal. She would hear that her husband hadn't really fallen in love with her after capturing her; he'd only been recruited by his opportunistic father to win her and the family over so that the treasure they'd created could be weaponized for his own gain. Winnie thought back to the day she'd met Tod for lunch, how he'd proclaimed his love for his wife and his regret at the terrible circumstances of their union. He'd told her then that he thought she'd have to die to stay with him as his partner and ally. That, at least, had been the truth: he'd been foolish enough to think her Elemental body would pass into the Depths just like a mortal's would. It turned Winnie's stomach to think that the only reason her sister hadn't been snuffed out of existence altogether was because of Damion Strife's intervention. If Strife hadn't kept Tod from killing Verna, Ren would never have been born. She hated the thought, but she owed Strife a debt of gratitude for that intervention, even if the truth of the matter was that Strife exploited the situation to his own advantage: preserving life had nothing to do with his decisions.

And how well Tod played his part! she thought bitterly. It was brilliant, really, the way he'd fooled them all into thinking he was trustworthy. And no one had been fooled more than Verna. Despite her exhaustion, Winnie felt fury swell in her gut: Tod would pay for what he'd done to her sister. He'd pay for robbing Renata of the security she deserved.

Ren...

How could a father do what Tod had done to his daughter? It was Tod's cruelest treachery: when the Harvesters had welcomed baby Ren, when they'd gazed at her and imagined the future she'd enjoy and the powers they'd nurture as she grew, Winnie had foolishly believed Tod was imagining those things too. But the truth was that he'd been scheming all along to mine those powers, unknown though they were at the time.

The Harvesters had seen Ren as a miracle; her father had seen the girl only as a weapon.

Winnie had opened her eyes then at the sound of snuffling behind Verna to see Pete and Brooke standing together, giving the sisters space to reunite before welcoming their granddaughter home again. Winnie managed a weak smile, but her body felt weary again at the thought of what they'd think when they learned the truth.

And her stomach had curdled when she'd considered the larger ramifications: Tod and Strife were angry and united. They'd had a plan to extend their powers far beyond the Depths. And Winnie may have been able to contain them for now, but how long would that last? How long would it be before they'd found a way to escape the Depths? What terrible plan would they be hatching in the meantime?

And despite the little rescue squad's vow to keep Ren's incredible power a secret for as long as they could, what would happen when they discovered, as they someday must, what that power was?

Surreptitiously, Winnie had reached up and removed her sunglasses, looking into her parents' tear-stained faces. Brooke's mouth had fallen open, and Pete had become dangerously still, his chin dropping and his countenance darkening as he looked at his oldest daughter's white eyes.

Did they know, as Strife had, what her new look meant? What would they think when they learned not only of Tod's betrayal but of Strife's apparent determination to start a war against the Others? It was one more difficult conversation Winnie had to add to the list.

Winnie had slipped Nolan's sunglasses back on and pulled away from her sister. She'd introduced Nolan, who also got a powerful hug from Verna and her repeated thanks, and then Verna had fussed briefly and perfunctorily over Nina, though it was clear her mind was utterly consumed by Ren.

When she'd released a very uncomfortable-looking Vita from an embrace that featured many thank-yous from Verna and a lot of back-patting and escape attempts from Vita, she looked around expectantly.

"Where's Tod?" she asked.

Winnie had opened her mouth to begin the first hard conversation she knew she was facing, but before she could say anything, Vita turned Verna by the shoulders and steered her back into the apartment.

"Winnie needs to get Nina and Nolan home; I'll fill you in on what happened while we were gone," she'd said, and Winnie had just enough time to mouth a grateful *thank you* to Vita before the door clicked shut behind them.

Now it was just the three of them before Nolan's building, exhausted, dirty, and dragging. Nina had agreed to stay with Nolan for the time being while she recuperated, and Winnie had vowed to be a frequent visitor. They all needed time to recover.

"You know what this means, right, Winnie?" Nina said, pushing her glass up her nose and sweeping her hair out of her face.

"Yes," Winnie said darkly. "It means that for the first time in hundreds and hundreds of years, my family and all the Others like us have an enemy. And I don't think Strife is going to give up trying to extend his power just because this plan fell through.

"And I think we may have an even bigger issue because when I was hugging Verna, I'm pretty sure I felt a suspicious bulge in her midsection..."

"Oh! Oh my gosh, Winnie," Nina exclaimed, reaching out to clutch Winnie's hand. "Yes, it means all of those things, too!"

Winnie looked at her quizzically. "Wait, what were you going to say?"

Nina raised her shoulders sheepishly. "I was going to say that I have to find a new job now."

Winnie stared at her friend blankly for several beats, and then she guffawed. She threw her arms around Nina, and the two women stood giggling together while Nolan looked on in bewilderment.

Winnie peeked up at him, and he rolled his eyes, but when she reached out a hand to him, he intertwined his fingers with hers and smiled, his warm gaze reflected in her opalescent eyes.

Acknowledgements

Thank you...

To George again, for predicting where the story was headed but refusing to let me confirm or deny along the way.

To JAKE, for occasionally being quiet. Just occasionally.

To Raquel Sotomayor, for giving Winnie eyes to see, and to Mark Kregger, for designing a cover for this book that showcases Raquel's art just perfectly.

To Kathleen Jowaski, for being even better at editing this time around than the last time we did this together.

To Alice, for risking a second first read.

To Dad, for being weirdly good at marketing and for talking up the first book to everyone. Literally everyone.

And to Winnie's fans, who asked for a second book, which is the loveliest compliment a character can receive. You're all just the best.